MW00415881

NORI'S DELTA (SPECIAL FORCES: OPERATION ALPHA)

DELTA TEAM 3, BOOK ONE

LORI RYAN

Dear Readers,

Welcome to the Special Forces: Operation Alpha Fan-Fiction world!

If you are new to this amazing world, in a nutshell the author wrote a story using one or more of my characters in it. Sometimes that character has a major role in the story, and other times they are only mentioned briefly. This is perfectly legal and allowable because they are going through Aces Press to publish the story.

This book is entirely the work of the author who wrote it. While I might have assisted with brainstorming and other ideas about which of my characters to use, I didn't have any part in the process or writing or editing the story.

I'm proud and excited that so many authors loved my characters enough that they wanted to write them into their own story. Thank you for supporting them, and me!

This series is special to me as the five authors writing in the Delta Team Three series took a team that I introduced in *Shielding Kinley* and made them their own.

READ ON!
Xoxo
Susan Stoker

CHAPTER 1

His body made it on the plane but he felt like his stomach was still on the ground somewhere. Which wasn't the least bit normal for him.

Heath Davis—known to his team and most everyone other than his dad and sisters as Woof—was the last to board the military transport set to take them to their next assignment. That was about all he knew so far. Waking up in the middle of the night and leaving for a mission with little or no notice came with the territory on Delta Team Three.

But he didn't usually have to deal with the fog that surrounded his brain on this particular night and the crap feeling in the pit of his stomach. Even though the team had been out drinking the night before with Trigger and his team, a team they worked with often and had just finished a mission with, he didn't expect to feel this way.

They'd met up with the guys at The Ugly Mug, a bar where they spent a lot of their down time. He probably shouldn't have matched Doc shot for shot. That had been mistake number one.

When Grover and Oz joined in, shit had gone to hell fast.

Trigger and Lefty had brought their women and, truth was, it hurt to see Trigger and Lefty there with the women they'd fallen hard for. Somehow, despite the kind of work they do, those guys had made it work for them. They'd found amazing women who were nothing like the flaky, vain barracks babes who often threw themselves at them in bars, wanting nothing more than to say they'd fucked a special forces guy.

Heath had once hoped he might have the kind of love his friends had found, but it wasn't looking like that was going to pan out for him.

So, yeah, he'd done something he hadn't done in a long time. He'd gotten tanked and he was paying for it.

He opened his go bag and grabbed one of the small baggies he kept in the side pocket and tossed a handful of vitamins and supplements in his mouth. If it was a hangover, they might not help. But if he was getting sick, he needed to head it off now before it snowballed.

His teammate Zip, a guy who was all-smiles, all the time, handed him a bottle of water that Woof promptly used to wash down the pills and capsules. Jangles shook his blond head at both of them.

"They won't save you," Jangles said.

2

"But they won't hurt," Woof and Zip said in near unison. They both believed in the power of vitamins and homeopathic remedies and the team didn't hold back on ribbing them on it.

Woof tipped his head back and finished the bottle of water. He knew the other thing that wouldn't hurt was hydrating. Hitting the Middle East without feeling like he was all there would only get worse if he was dehydrated.

Merlin sank onto the bench beside Jangles, with Duff settling onto the bench across from them, rounding out the team. Merlin was the old man among them at thirty-five. Not that that was old, but his hair was starting to gray around the edges and there was no way in hell they weren't going to point that out to him any chance they got.

Duff didn't say anything, only gave a nod to each of them. He didn't ever say all that much, though. He was a big son-of-a-bitch and if his size wasn't enough to scare off most people, his personality was. He made a scrub brush look soft and cuddly. Come to think of it, he made a scrub brush look chatty, too. But he was one of the team and the men were loyal to the core to him, same as he was to them.

Merlin passed a heavily encased tablet around the group. "We're heading in to grab Eleanor Bonham at the Adana airport in Turkey. She's the Associate Counselor for the US Department of State. We're going to escort her into the Republic of Kazarus for a covert meeting with Onur Demir."

Woof rested his arms on his knees and leaned forward. "Head of the Kazarus Freedom Army?"

Merlin gave a nod as Jangles passed the tablet on to Zip.

"She's been tasked with negotiating a covert agreement with the KFA. We support them off the books and, if they're successful in overthrowing the current regime, they'll support our efforts against Al Qaeda and ISIS," Merlin said. "We've got intel that the Kazarus government has been feeding weapons to the terrorist organizations and that shit has to stop. This is one of the ways our guys are attempting to cut off that pipeline."

They all knew Al Qaeda and ISIS had begun working together lately. Each organization had been hit hard by the US and their allies in the Middle East, but if they were successful in banding together, the strides that had been made against them lately might be wiped out.

"Kazarus has never been particularly stable," Woof said.

"No, it hasn't," Merlin agreed. When one of its surrounding nations wasn't controlling it, Kazarus had been rife with bloodshed and civil war.

The current government was an absolute monarchy with the king, Ehsan Barrera, at the helm with his eight sons in line for the throne. The family had been in place for the past twenty-five years and didn't seem inclined to give up their hold on the country and the small iron and oil reserves the land boasted.

"Demir and his rebel army claim to want to put a democracy in place. Our government wants to gamble on backing them if the terms are right," Merlin said.

Woof took the tablet Zip handed him but didn't look down at it yet. "Demir's group has taken hostages in the past."

Jangles was the one to answer this time. "They have. They're still holding two doctors and three nurses from the US, England, and France hostage. It's a complication."

No one said anything. It wasn't their job to question the decisions made by the people who told them what to do. They got their orders and they followed them. The person negotiating with Demir would need to walk that tightrope since the US didn't make concessions where hostages were concerned.

Woof looked down at the tablet and lost his breath. Lost was the wrong word. It was knocked clean the hell out of him. He looked into the serious face of a slight woman in a suit gazing back at him with challenge and determination in her eyes.

Long straight brown hair framed hazel eyes and a mouth held in a flat line as she looked into the camera. He knew those eyes. There was a time when he'd been able to bring a smile to them and a curve to that stiff mouth, and he'd reveled in doing just that. In knowing he was the one who could do that to her.

That and other things. He shifted in his seat, his body going rock hard at the memories. That was a long-damned time ago, back when they were kids and he'd been innocent enough to believe nothing could touch him. Touch them. So damned naïve.

It wasn't a surprise it had all gone to shit.

He blinked as he processed that her name had changed and looked back at the name on the file. Eleanor Bonham.

She'd been Eleanor Duncan when he knew her.

Well, damn, if that didn't kick him in the gut. Not that it should.

It should mean nothing to him that Nori had gotten married. He hadn't seen her in fifteen years. Of course she'd moved on and gotten married, built a life for herself. He wouldn't let himself wonder if she had children. If she was happy. There was no point in going there.

She was a mission and the mission was all that mattered.

Yeah. Sure. He knew bullshit when he heard it and that was all he was spouting now.

He moved his gaze back to Merlin's. "Credible threat or standard protection detail?"

"There's been chatter about going after her to put a stop to the meeting. Nothing concrete yet and we aren't sure who's focused on her, but we'll take it seriously anyway."

Woof nodded. Damned right they would. He felt the same deep ache in his chest he'd felt when things had ended so long ago with Eleanor. She wouldn't be happy to see him, but he wouldn't let that keep him from making sure she got in and out of the fractious country and back to her husband without a scratch on her.

He had failed to protect Eleanor before, but things would be different this time. He wasn't good for much in this world, but he was damned good at what he did for the military. And he'd make sure that skill was put to good use here. If Eleanor was headed into danger, he'd be there to see her through it.

CHAPTER 2

Eleanor didn't bother to stop at the baggage carousels. She had one carry-on she was rolling behind her and an overnight bag slung over a shoulder. And she was still trying to cram her notes into the side pocket of said bag.

If her assistant was with her, she'd have handed the notes to her to put in the immaculately organized accordion file Beth kept with her at all times. There would be tabs and notes and everything cross referenced for Eleanor. But Beth would be coming in on a flight two hours from now so until then, Eleanor was on her own.

Truth be told, she was normally more organized than this herself, but flying always got to her. It was the one part of her job she didn't love.

Eleanor could have had a car take her ahead to the base, but she didn't much see the point in that when she could just as easily find a seat here and work while she waited the short time for Beth. They'd travel to the base together and meet up with the rest of the people that would be going into this negotiation with her.

She'd chosen people she had worked with in the past and trusted to be her support team. Marcus was a fantastic analyst and was easy to work with. He was younger than the others in the group, but his boyish, blond good looks belied a quick mind.

Geoff could be as prickly as his salt and pepper beard, but his mind was sharp and she liked the way he could break down issues with ease when they were in the middle of a situation.

Sharon was one of the fastest researchers they had in their office and Eleanor knew she might need that kind of talent when dealing with Onur Demir.

Her stomach flipped again and this time it wasn't the dregs of motion sickness from the flight. It was the thought of the negotiation.

It wasn't that she was nervous about it. It was just that she knew this was a make or break moment for her career. Normally her boss would handle this, but there were timing constraints involved and her boss was in Europe meeting with the leaders of three nations whose support was crucial to the success of several US endeavors going forward.

Eleanor spotted a chair in the far corner of the long room, well past the noise and chaos of the baggage pickup. It was just the type of quiet spot she needed. If she put her headphones on and focused on the upcoming meeting, she'd get just as much done there as she would if she went to the base.

She'd settle in and then let Beth know where to find her.

"Ms. Bonham!"

Eleanor slowed and searched for the sound of the voice. A man in fatigue pants and a buttoned-down shirt with rolled sleeves approached holding out an ID card.

"I'm glad I found you. I was worried I wouldn't be able to," he said in heavily accented English.

"Can I help you?" Eleanor shifted the bag on her shoulder and faced the man.

"I've been sent to pick you up. Your assistant's flight was moved up so she arrived earlier and was taken to the base already. We are to meet her and the rest of your team there."

Eleanor studied his ID card, looking up to be sure his face matched. She nodded and switched her trajectory, following the man toward the doors heading outside. She'd planned to review the file on Onur Demir while she waited for Beth, but she could do that while the man drove. Hopefully he'd let her work in peace. Most of the time, if she didn't start up a conversation and gave only short answers to any attempts from the other person, she could get people to leave her alone pretty quickly.

She pulled her phone out as she followed the man.

She could at least check messages quickly before they got in the car. The man was guiding her through the crowd, talking about the need to hurry to the base before night fell, though she didn't know why. Adana wasn't a dangerous city, as far as she knew.

She kept one eye on the path the man was making for her as they made their way along the walkway and slid her thumb over her messages.

"Ma'am, we should get to the car. There is time for that once we're on the road."

Eleanor wanted to roll her eyes but didn't. Like she couldn't walk and read at the same time.

As the crowd fell away behind them and they moved further along the walkway to a more isolated area, she opened a message from Beth and read the lines. Beth's flight was delayed four hours and she wouldn't be in until the evening. She said that Eleanor should go along to the base without her.

Eleanor's steps faltered as she looked at the time the message was sent. Ten minutes ago.

So why had the man said her assistant was already at the base?

She looked over at the man at her side and slowed, moving away. "I've just realized I should really use the bathroom before we go."

He shook his head. "There's no time for that." He reached for her arm, but she stepped back.

"I'll be fast. If I don't go now—"

He didn't let her finish. This time when he reached

for her, he caught his mark, his face going dark as he grabbed her with enough force to leave a bruise.

Eleanor's heart slammed into overdrive and she felt a rush of panic and fear overtake her. Why hadn't she called the base to confirm his identity? She knew better than that. Any change in plans should be confirmed in her job. But she'd been so focused on trying to prep for the role ahead of her that she hadn't thought. Hadn't stopped to take the time to do what she knew she should. And now she was going to pay for that mistake.

Fear kicked her into action and her self-defense training kicked in. She dropped her bags and twisted, wrenching her arm up and close to her body to pull the man off balance. He kept his hold on her but it had loosened. She turned into him and raised her foot, bringing it down on his knee at an angle. He let out a cry and she shoved as hard as she could before turning to bolt.

She ran, then, ignoring his shouts as she tried to get back to the busy section of the airport where she might get help. Blood rushed in her ears and she couldn't get her body to move fast enough. It felt like she was swimming through mud with concrete blocks where her feet should be.

It was then that she realized there was more than just his shouting she was hearing. Someone else was calling to her. Eleanor looked up to see three large men running at her and she froze.

These guys weren't like the man she'd just escaped

from. With his medium height and build, he'd been hard enough to evade, even with the training she'd had. These men were a different story altogether.

If these men got hold of her, she'd be done. Each of them was bigger than a truck, well-muscled, and from the looks of them, a hell of a lot more skilled than the man behind her. It was in the way they moved. That loose-hipped swagger that said they knew damned well how to take apart anyone who got in their way. The confidence that oozed off of them, telling the world to move out of their way, or else. And it was an *or else* they were fully capable of following through on.

She needed to move. Now!

She couldn't go backward so she swerved and headed toward the side of the terminal. Maybe she could evade them until she made it back toward the crowd and then lose them somehow in the fray.

Part of her knew that wasn't remotely possible, but she wasn't about to stop trying. She had to keep moving. If she didn't, they would get her and this—whatever *this* was—would end badly.

"Eleanor!"

Her lungs burned and she knew she was sucking in air way too fast. She was going to hyperventilate.

"Nori stop!"

This time, something about the shouted name began to chisel through the terror and panic. No one called her Nori.

At least not anymore.

Before she could piece together the disjointed memory of another time and place with what was happening here, she lost her footing. Her shoe caught on something and she was falling.

"Nori stop!" came the instruction again, command behind the tone.

Eleanor couldn't stop. She pitched forward, putting her arms out as the ground rushed toward her.

But she didn't land on the concrete as she thought she would. Strong arms caught her. She began to kick and punch out at the man who held her, knowing that to give in would mean they'd have her. If they got her away from here, she'd never get away. Hell, it might mean her death. She didn't face danger every day in her job, but there was always the possibility of it.

"Nori, it's Heath. It's Heath Davis. I've got you. I've got you."

Eleanor froze again as his words broke through the haze surrounding her. Heath?

She couldn't make sense of the name, so out of place in her world now. So unexpected.

She looked up into the glass-green eyes of a man she never thought she'd see again. And certainly not in the middle of a kidnapping attempt outside a Turkish airport.

Whether it was the stress of the moment, the shock of seeing him again, or the insanity that now seemed to be firmly taking over her battered mind, she let out a garbled half-laugh, half-cry. Then she did the only thing she could in that moment.

She let herself slump into the hold of a man she'd once thought she'd loved. Once, a very long time ago when she was a very different person.

CHAPTER 3

He didn't think Eleanor was fully processing what was happening.

"Principal is secured. Pursuing target," Jangles said through their comms as he and Zip took off after the guy who'd just tried to grab Eleanor.

Heath had his arm around her and was practically carrying her as he took in their surroundings. There was no sign of anyone else working with the man. No one who looked like they would be a threat. Only shocked onlookers who had realized too late that something was happening.

He scooped up her bags where she'd dropped them and looked down at Eleanor. Her eyes were glassy and he could feel her shaking.

He spoke quietly, his voice low and reassuring. "You're all right now, Nori. They won't get near you now that we're here."

He'd said much the same thing a few times now and she nodded jerkily but he knew she'd need time to deal with what had just happened.

Thank fuck he'd gotten to her in time. He didn't want to think what might have happened if the man had gotten her away from the terminal to someplace he could work her over alone. Heath had seen too much of what people could do to each other in this world.

She tilted up her head to look at him. "Why are you here?"

She took a little step back as she seemed to realize how close they were. He didn't blame her. He was probably the last person she wanted to see.

"I'll explain it all when we get you into a vehicle."

She looked down the sidewalk at all the cars coming through the passenger pickup line closer to the terminal.

"My team will be here any—"

He stopped when Merlin pulled their SUV around the traffic of the airport, two wheels kissing the curb, before coming to a stop in front of them. Heath nudged her to the car, steering her to the back seat and then sliding in beside her so she was sandwiched between him and Duff.

Jangles and Zip jogged up to the car, Zip jumping into the front seat, while Jangles hopped into the third row through the back.

"I take it you didn't catch up to the guy who tried to grab her?" Heath was talking through gritted teeth but he couldn't stop himself. He was trying to deal with the insane protective drive coursing through him at seeing her in danger just now.

It wasn't anything like dealing with protection detail on another op. There were plenty of times when a threat got up close and personal with their principal. They handled it. Stayed calm and got the job done, neutralizing the danger.

When Heath saw Eleanor struggling with that man, saw that man's hands on her, cold hard rage had torn through his body so hard and fast it damn near floored him. He'd be damned if he was going to let anything happen to this woman.

Zip turned in his seat, answering Heath's question about the man they'd been chasing. "Took a header right over the edge of the overpass before we could grab him. Actually dove headfirst like he wanted to make damned sure he didn't survive that fall."

Heath saw Eleanor go pale as she wrapped her arms around her middle and seemed to gulp in air. Damn. He needed to settle her down. He put a hand on her leg and squeezed gently, focusing her attention on him.

Heath spoke quietly. "Slow your breathing. Nice and easy."

She watched him as she did as he said, taking one deep breath after another.

"Eleanor, this is Merlin." Heath gestured to Merlin who was currently pulling the car away from the curb and out into traffic.

Sirens sounded in the distance.

"Step on it, Mer." This came from Zip.

"That's Zip," Heath said as Zip grinned and waved. Zip was always smiling. They could be knee deep in shit with a shit storm brewing and more shit headed at them on a tidal wave, and that man would grin and talk about how much he loved shit.

He gestured to Duff who sat on the other side of her. "This is Duff." To her credit, she didn't blink at the size of the enormous man or the fact he wore a perpetual glower on his face as she turned and nodded her greeting.

"Jangles is in the back," he said tipping his head toward the only blond on their team. Jangles had his head in a laptop and Heath would guess he was working on deleting video footage from the airport, but he looked up and nodded at Eleanor.

Heath returned his gaze to Eleanor, watching her as he spoke to see if her heart rate and breathing were starting to return to normal. He could no longer see the small vein in her neck pumping and she wasn't gulping for air like she had been. That was good.

He had to give her credit. She had calmed herself faster than a lot of people would in that situation.

"We've been assigned to protect you. We're going to make sure you get to the meeting with Demir on time and in one piece," Heath said, willing himself to be professional where this woman was concerned. What he wanted to do was haul her into his lap and hold her till her shaking stopped.

"On time, every time." This quip came from Jangles. "That's our motto." He didn't look up from the laptop as he spoke.

"I'm pretty sure that's taken already. Some moving company or insurance company or something," said Duff.

"Damn, should've trademarked that shit when we had the chance," Jangles said. He shut the laptop. "Video's scrubbed," he said, letting them all know he'd erased any airport security video of what had just gone down.

Heath could see the wheels turning in Eleanor's head. She was smart, she would put it all together quickly, he was sure.

"You went into the Army," she said, "but you guys have to be special forces. Rangers? Green Berets?" She tilted her head, studying him and he could guess she was taking in the longer hair and the scruff on his chin. Someone in her position would know special forces were allowed a lot more leeway in their appearance than your average soldier. "Delta?"

He shook his head. "Can't discuss that."

She rolled her eyes and he knew she was thinking of her security clearance. As Delta forces, they had top secret clearance, but so did she. In fact, she probably had a few ticks higher than that, but they still didn't need to discuss who and what his team was. It just wasn't something they did unless they had to.

Eleanor seemed to move on then, accepting his response. "He said my assistant had already landed, but she hadn't." She tensed beside him, sitting up straighter. "My team is on their way here. Will these people go after them? Are they safe?"

He reassured her. "There's another team grabbing them. They'll take them to Kazarus using a different route and we'll meet up with them just ahead of the summit with Demir."

"I'm supposed to go to the US Air Force base here in Adana." Eleanor shifted around to look around them at the roads outside the car. "I have to get to the meet with Demir. It's too important not to."

"We'll get you there," Heath said quietly.

"Just going to have a change of plans, mix things up a little," said Merlin from the front seat. "Someone fed them your itinerary. We need to change things up to keep you safe. From now on, no one outside this car is going to know our plans or your itinerary."

Eleanor gave another of those too-jerky nods and he saw her press her hands to her thighs to control the shaking that had started moments before. "Why did they want me? Where was he planning to take me?"

There was a stillness in the car at her question and she looked to Heath, searching his expression. He stayed carefully neutral.

"We don't know for sure but there's been some chatter someone wants to make sure you don't make it to this meeting. Could be the Kazarus government. Could be members of the terrorist groups in this region that have an interest in keeping that regime in place. Could be any number of organizations, but we know one thing: he wasn't planning to take you home for tea and cookies."

He didn't mention the possibilities. It was possible they would have held her for a time and then let her go, but the more likely scenario was that they would have taken her someplace off the grid and killed her outright. If the US couldn't get a negotiator to Demir alive, they might just have to give up on the idea of forming an alliance with him.

Eleanor looked down at her hands and he could see her working to absorb the shock. She might be high up in the foreign service, but anyone who wasn't used to dealing with the scum of the earth like this on a daily basis would be hit hard when it came so close to home.

Heath vowed to himself he'd put a stop to whatever assholes were trying to hurt her. He'd failed her before, but he'd be damned if he'd ever let that happen again. She would be safe with him and his team.

She had to be.

CHAPTER 4

"We'll get some sleep here while the guys grab provisions and make arrangements for the next leg of our trip," Heath said, putting Eleanor's bag on the small bed in the equally small apartment.

Eleanor had watched as he and the others checked the room before the other men on the team filed out without a word. It seemed like they all had some strange ability to communicate with each other without words. Or maybe this was standard operating procedure or whatever and they didn't need to talk through a plan before acting. It probably wasn't unusual for them to be protecting someone who'd just had an attempt made on her life so they had to go through the motions.

She was beginning to realize that's what had happened back there at the airport. The man might have been trying to kidnap her, but more than likely given what Heath had said, the end goal was to kill her and dump her body somewhere she'd never be found.

A chill ran through her for what seemed like the hundredth time that day and she rubbed her arms to try to chase away the sensation.

And then Heath was there in front of her pulling her into his arms and rubbing her back with those large warm hands and it felt so damned right. So safe.

This was Heath. *Her* Heath, the boy she'd dated in her last year of high school. From another lifetime, it seemed.

The boy she'd hurt in more ways than she could count.

She forced back the memories, trying to focus on the here and now. She wasn't that girl anymore. She wasn't weak and insecure and afraid the way she had been so often then.

And truth be told, she could see he was different than he was in high school. He'd been smiling and happy all the time then, but it was an act. He'd used jokes to deflect what he was feeling. Now, he might joke with his team, but he was changed on a basic level. He was hardened with an edge to him that said he'd seen and done things no ordinary person would want to know about.

There was genuine confidence about him now, too. Not the bravado of a kid jock who put on a show for everyone around him. This was the kind of certainty that said he knew who he was and what he had to contribute to the world. That said he wasn't worried about what people thought of him.

Not to mention, he was very different physically. The boy had filled out. He was taller. Maybe 6-foot-2 and all muscle. His light brown hair reached his shoulders and his tanned, chiseled jaw was covered in a beard and mustache she wanted to run her fingers through. He had a small scar at his temple and another cutting across the left side of his lip. The green eyes she'd always loved looked at her softly now as he continued to tell her to breathe.

Lust slammed into her just as it always had where he was concerned. Talk about wrong place and wrong time. And definitely wrong person.

She gave herself a minute to sink into the heat of his embrace, to melt and let the fear and tension of all that had happened melt away. But then she reminded herself she had no right to take any comfort from this man. Not to mention, they were in the middle of trying to get her to a very important negotiation. One she couldn't mess up or muddle with distractions.

She stepped back and broke the embrace. She should have her mind on her work. She had known coming into these talks that this was going to be messy. The United States had always had a strict policy of not negotiating for hostages. And while that was still the case, they now made the distinction between negotiation for hostages and communicating with them.

So she was being sent in to talk to Onur Demir

about other things, but discussing the health and well-being of those hostages wasn't out of the question. And stressing to him that her government would be more likely to broker a deal with him for support of his cause if those hostages were released wouldn't violate protocol.

Of course, that got messy and there were plenty of people back home who thought she shouldn't be here. But she went where the President and her State Department bosses told her to go, and they'd told her to come talk to Demir.

Heath's voice when he broke into her thoughts was raspy but there was a gentleness to it. "You should get some sleep, Nori. We need to move again soon and you'll feel better if you get some rest before then."

"Eleanor," she said.

"What?"

She lifted her head to meet his gaze. "Eleanor. No one calls me Nori anymore."

His grin was slow and so damned sexy she almost forgot for a minute that fifteen years had passed since they'd seen each other. That she had no claim on this man anymore. No right to be thinking the things she was thinking about him. No right to feel the reaction her body was having to his touch.

"Eleanor, then," he said softly.

His words were simple, but they snapped her back to reality and she stepped away from him. She wasn't Nori and they weren't in high school anymore.

She was Eleanor Bonham. She worked for the State Department and she was about to negotiate an agreement that could mean the difference between maintaining the strides they'd made in the fight on terror or losing it all.

It was probably silly, but the recitation of who and what she was, grounded her. She crossed to the bed but stared at the mattress instead of laying down. "I don't think I can sleep."

She sank to the floor in front of the bed, leaning her head back and closing her eyes. She heard more than felt him come and settle beside her. Even as he sat, he was still on duty, on guard. She could tell.

It was more than just the fact that he still had knives and guns strapped to him in more places than she could count. It was the way he was constantly scanning even the small space around them. It was the way she could tell he had an ear cocked to the outside even as he seemed to give her his attention.

"Don't worry, Eleanor. We're going to get you in and out of this summit with Demir and get you home to your family. I won't let anything happen to you."

She didn't reply but she felt the tightening in her gut at his words. She didn't have a family to go home to. Not really, anyway. But that wasn't a conversation she wanted to have right now.

"So, what are the others out there doing? You said they need a plan. There's no plan for how you're going to get me across the border into Kazarus?" She stood again as she spoke, walking the few paces to the other side of the room before turning and walking back.

Shouldn't elite forces like his have plans with backup plans, and then some?

If he was bothered by her questions, he didn't show it. Then again, she had the feeling he didn't let anyone see anything he didn't want them to see.

The man before her was highly disciplined and clearly every bit the elite warrior special forces were said to be. Pride at who he'd become swelled through her. Not that she'd had anything to do with it, but still. He was clearly damned good at what he did.

"We know where we're headed and how we're going to get there. We need to set some things in motion on the ground to implement those plans." He leveled her with a look. "And we'll be setting up a few decoy plans as well, giving whoever is gunning for you something else to chase for a while."

His phone buzzed and he looked at the screen before looking back to her. "Your assistant and the rest of your team are safe."

Eleanor felt a rush of relief at the news. Not that they all didn't go into this work knowing the risks, but still, she wouldn't forgive herself if anything happened to them because someone was trying to kill her.

"Who has them? You said it was another Delta Team?"

He shook his head, tapping back something on the screen before turning his attention to her. "I said no such thing. Stop putting words into my mouth." He grinned her way. "But, yeah, another team has them. We've worked with these guys before. One of them, Ris, was a buddy of mine when I was in Ranger school."

"Ranger school? So you're a Ranger?"

"Once a Ranger, always a Ranger."

She had a feeling if she was any other person they were protecting, he'd be saying nothing, but he seemed to be playing with her and she had a feeling she'd get the information out of him soon. They would have gotten a dossier on her when they got the assignment. He knew she meant it when she said her clearance was higher than his.

Even so, he was being vague. It was in a special forces operative's blood not to reveal who they were and what their assignments were.

Eleanor watched him carefully. He didn't seem to hate his life. Didn't seem miserable with his decision to enter the Army. Since she was the reason he'd had to make that decision, it mattered to her.

She sat on the floor next to him again and stretched her legs out in front of them. She wanted to lean into him, letting him put his arm around her like he had when they were young, but she didn't. She still felt the constant hum of arousal when she was near him and that just irritated the hell out of her.

She wasn't like that. She wasn't the kind of woman who let attraction distract her from her job. Not to mention, it was stupid for her body to be even remotely aware of anyone of the opposite sex at a time like this. She needed to get her shit together.

She focused on what he'd just said. "Ris and you were Rangers together?"

She didn't get to hear the answer to that question. Heath went tight and sat up, motioning her to be quiet.

In a heartbeat, he sprang into action, throwing himself over her and pushing her to the ground as what sounded like an explosion came from the front of the apartment.

Eleanor screamed and covered her ears, but she was too late to stop the ringing. Heath put an arm around her waist and hauled her up at the same time she saw his other arm come up with a gun trained on the door. He shoved her behind him as gunfire rang out.

When shards of wood exploded out of the window frame behind her she realized it wasn't only Heath's weapon she was hearing.

No, all that noise couldn't come from one weapon. Eleanor watched in horror as four men flooded the small space between Heath and her. She was equally horrified when two of those men fell to Heath's bullets.

Heath lifted the bed they'd been leaning on moments before with one arm and she realized it was little more than a cot with a mattress. He shoved it on its side in front of them, giving them the barest bit of cover.

"The window!" Heath kept himself between Eleanor

and the men firing as he pushed her back to the window. "Open it and go out on the fire escape!"

"What about you?"

She thought she almost heard a smirk in his voice when he answered her with a "Right behind you, babe."

Her hands fumbled and she flinched again and again as she shoved open the windowpane. Then she was climbing through it and he was moving behind her.

She heard Heath grunt in pain and she was pushed to the metal floor of the fire escape as he fell on top of her. She heard the sickening thud of his head hitting the metal railing.

"Oh God, Heath!"

There was blood. A lot of it. His forehead was bleeding and his left arm was drenched in blood where he'd been shot.

He'd been shot and she was alone here with at least one or maybe two men with guns coming for her.

She shifted her body so she was out from under the weight of him and reached for his gun. She hadn't had more than training at the range, though she'd put in enough hours there to know how to handle the weapon.

But she'd sure as hell never fired a gun at another human being. Still she'd be damned if she was going to sit and wait to die.

Or watch them kill this man who'd saved her, who

had put his life on the line for her security. The man she'd once loved with all her heart.

She lifted the weapon and trained her aim on the window while she tried shaking Heath awake with her other hand. She needed him. They were in a seedy part of town in a city she'd only ever driven through as a passenger before. She didn't have a clue where to go from here. She had no idea how to reach his team. She didn't know where to go if she got them off this fire escape.

And that was a huge if. How the hell did she think she was going to be able to lift this man? She couldn't. And she sure as hell couldn't climb down a ladder with him.

Sirens sounded in the distance and she was reminded of the sirens she'd heard at the airport. They were too far away to help her now, just as they had been then.

And something told her this time, there would be no shouts from a Delta team coming in the nick of time to save her. She took a steadying breath, resisting the urge to try to wake up Heath. She needed to be ready when their attackers came through that window.

The window filled with the dark shape of a man and time seemed to slow as she saw the weapon in his hand. Saw him raise it and point it at her and she was frozen in fear for the briefest second. She only hoped that wasn't enough to cost her. To cost Heath.

She squeezed the trigger, aiming for center body

mass as she'd been taught during all those sessions her stepdad had paid for when she joined the foreign service.

The gun was a lot bigger than she was used to so it was no surprise when it sent her body jerking back. She didn't stop firing, though. Two, three, four times. Until the man slumped over the window.

Her heart beat a wild rhythm in her chest and she didn't let herself think about the fact she probably just killed this man. She couldn't face that right now. Not on top of everything else.

Heath groaned and shifted and she shook him again.

"Heath! Open your eyes, Heath! Please!"

He groaned once more and then he was sitting, taking in the scene around them and assessing things as though he wasn't bleeding from the head and arm. That's apparently what special forces training would do for you.

He pulled another gun from somewhere on his body and crouched in front of her, waiting. His response when the next man came to the window was so fast, she didn't see him move. He fired off two shots and the man fell, disappearing beneath the window.

"Let's go," Heath said, taking both guns and pushing her in front of him again, toward the ladder that led to the ground.

And then they were moving through alleys and in and out of buildings. Eleanor thought he was being overly cautious. She'd seen four men come into the apartment and all of those men were dead now. There were sirens telling her the police were coming in response to the gunfire. Surely, no one else would come after them now.

She was wrong. She heard the shouts of two men behind them and looked back to see them at the end of the busy street. They were clearly looking for someone and she had a feeling it was Heath and her.

Heath took them through a market and into a small internet café where no one even bothered to look up from their screens when they entered. No one seemed to care when they slipped out the back door either. He kept them moving, not looking back.

By the time he pulled her into a dark bar, Eleanor's head was spinning. It took her a minute to realize they were in some kind of strip club. The women weren't as scantily clad as they might be in a US club but there were two women dancing in the center of the room and she saw women seated in men's laps here and there, grinding in the darkened corners.

He led her to a table in a corner near the back of the space. She realized then that he'd been talking for the last few minutes and could only guess he was talking to his team on some kind of comm system.

Heath sank into a seat at the table and Eleanor got her first good look at him. He was struggling. His eyes were glassy and he was breathing heavy. He looked up at her and pressed one of his guns into her hand under the table.

"Eleanor. My guys are going to come get you." He tipped his head toward a hallway. "You go down this hall and wait just inside the back door. They'll come down the alley and grab you."

She shook her head.

His eyes went hard and dark and she guessed she was supposed to be afraid. "I'm staying here to cover you if these guys come in here. Now, go!"

Eleanor shook her head. No way in hell was he leaving him here.

"I'll be right behind you Eleanor, I promise. I'll cover you from here and then I'm right behind you."

It was bullshit and she knew it. Hell, they both knew it. His left arm was hanging by his side and he looked like he might pass out again at any minute.

The front door opened. Eleanor didn't look to see if it was their pursuers. She grabbed a scarf someone had left sitting over the back of a chair and put it over her head. Then she straddled Heath in the chair and bent her head to kiss him, keeping her hands twined in the scarf as she wrapped her arms around him, so that anyone looking at them in the darkened corner would only see two people who should be renting a room instead of two people running from hired killers.

Heath groaned and gripped her hips and she thought for a minute he would push her off of him and force her to go out the back without her.

Fat chance in hell of that happening. He was only there because of her—in more ways than one. If she got him killed, she'd never forgive herself.

Then he was kissing her back and it was her turn to groan as need and hunger flooded her. God, this man had made her melt and forget all reason when they were in high school. He'd always been able to have her aroused and losing her mind with nothing more than his hands and mouth.

Now, though—now was a whole other story. His hands gripped her tight and pulled her hips to his. She felt all the strength of his hard body heating her own to the core. His mouth slanted over hers and he took control of the kiss, delving into her mouth and feasting on her with a passion that stole her breath.

She pressed her breasts to his chest as a slow sweet ache spread through her. She shouldn't be doing this. *They* shouldn't be doing this. It was all sorts of wrong, but damn if it didn't feel right.

She moaned against his lips, wanting nothing more than to stay in his arms.

Heath broke the kiss and she felt his glare on her for a second before he looked over her shoulder.

"They're gone."

Eleanor's cheeks heated as she realized he hadn't been affected by the kiss at all. He was still on, still working, making sure they were safe.

While she'd been acting like they were teenagers again in the back of his dad's BMW.

"You have to listen to me if I'm going to keep you safe, Eleanor."

She scrambled off his lap and stood. "I'm not going out the back without you so you need to find a way to stand up and move."

He grunted and pushed himself up, leaning heavily with his good arm on the table. His eyes seemed a little clearer, and she hoped the blow to the head was wearing off some. Eleanor put herself under his other arm and tried to support him, though she honestly didn't know if she was doing any good. Together, though, they moved down the hall he'd gestured to before. She could see the door he'd said to go through. Heath stumbled and pulled them off balance into the wall.

Eleanor pulled at him, getting him back to his feet again. Ten more feet and they'd be there, ready to go when his team came through for them.

Eight feet.

He stumbled again. Eleanor felt warm liquid running down her shoulder and it dawned on her that he was bleeding a lot more than she'd thought. Between that and the head wound, she didn't know how he was moving.

Six feet.

She put her all into getting him down that hall to the door. She had no idea if his team would come in to find them if they drove by and they didn't come out. Or maybe this was like the movies and if they didn't make this pickup point, they'd have to get to another one.

She couldn't get him to another one.

Heath slumped again and she let him go to the floor this time, leaning him against the wall and praying no one came back here and found them.

She ran the last few feet to the door and slammed it open before realizing that was stupid. He'd said to watch from the inside until his team came. She could just as easily stumble upon the men coming after her back there.

The alley was empty, though, and she looked back to Heath.

Damn.

She went back and grabbed him under the shoulders and tried to pull. That wasn't going to happen. The man was all muscle and she was not.

She ran back to the door and looked out. An SUV turned into the small space and headed for her. She shaded her eyes against the glare of the headlights and prayed it was his team and not the killers.

"Please, please, please." She looked back at Heath. He was pushing to his feet again, shaking his head. He took a stumbling step her way.

"Go Eleanor. It's them. Go!"

There was nothing in his tone that gave her room to argue or hesitate. It was an order plain and simple. She opened the door wide and stepped outside praying to God he was right and it was his team.

And then the car doors opened and Jangles and Zip spilled out.

"Heath is hurt. He needs help," she said, pulling back when Zip reached for her.

"Jangles has him. We need to get you out of here."

Still, she resisted until she saw Jangles coming out of the back door with Heath leaning heavily on him.

The idiot was grinning at her. Grinning like he'd just had the time of his life. And as Zip pulled her into the car, Heath winked at her like he used to when they were younger. And her stupid heart did a flip just like it did back then. More than it did back then, if she was honest.

As they tore out of the alley, she let herself sink into the back seat of the car and closed her eyes.

And thought about that kiss.

CHAPTER 5

Heath cursed as Zip put the last of the stitches into his head. He'd hit his head harder than he wanted to admit to his guys.

"Want to tell us how the hell you know our principal, Woof? And why the fuck you didn't think to mention this before the op?" Merlin was pissed and wasn't bothering to hide it.

Heath didn't blame him. He should have told them who Eleanor was the minute he'd recognized her picture. He wouldn't apologize, though. They might have pulled him from the mission and he wasn't going to trust Eleanor's safety to anyone but himself. Hell no on that score. He owed her that much.

"We dated in high school. Not a big deal." It was only a partial truth and he all but flinched as it came out of his mouth. These guys were his brothers. His team. They deserved the truth.

Zip snorted and Jangles was grinning like a fool. Duff looked about as amused as Merlin, which was not at all.

"Yeah that looked like a whole lot of no big deal the way you were rubbing her leg in the car." Zip made kissing noises and rubbed his own leg. "Let me find an excuse to touch your body, *Nori*. Let me rub you all over, *Nori*."

Heath growled. "She was hyperventilating, assclown." The last thing he needed was Eleanor waking up and hearing this.

He looked to where she slept, her head leaning on the seat. He wanted to pull her over to lean on his good arm instead, but he couldn't exactly pull that shit in front of his team now.

Merlin shot him a look in the rearview mirror. "You gonna be able to handle this without letting your past get in the way of the op?"

"Fuck you for asking," Heath bit out.

Merlin raised his hands off the wheel in surrender for a minute before putting them back. "Had to ask. We can't let you go into this if you're compromised, if your feelings are going to fuck this shit up. We need to get her in and out of there in one piece."

Heath's stomach pitched and it wasn't just because of the concussion he was walking around with. He didn't like thinking of anything happening to Eleanor.

"Trust me," he said, "I'm the last person who's going to let anything happen to her. I've got this."

Merlin was watching him and he could hear the weighted quiet in the back of the car, but it didn't take but a minute for the men to let him know they had his back.

"Okay," Merlin said. "Then we're behind you. We'll get her through this."

Heath nodded, his teeth still locked together. They had to—there was no other option but to get her through this and get her back home to safety. And knowing his team was behind him on this, behind her, made all the difference in the world.

*   *   *

Eleanor was drifting in and out of sleep. She should be getting herself ready for the meetings she would have with Onur Demir. You didn't walk into a negotiation with the head of a rebel guerrilla organization without being one hundred percent ready for any and all eventualities.

But her body had been pushed past all limits in the last twenty-four hours and she needed to sleep.

"She saved my ass back there."

Eleanor heard Heath talking through a fog. The response from the driver's seat was muffled.

"I was knocked out cold on the fire escape outside the building. If she hadn't had the wherewithal to pick up my gun and be ready for them, we would have both been sitting ducks out there."

"She's pretty amazing," Zip said beside her. "You think she can pull off this negotiation with Demir?"

"If anyone can, she can," Heath said.

Eleanor made to sit up. They were right to be focused on the negotiation. She needed to be focused on that too.

She didn't make it to sitting. Her eyes just didn't want to open.

She heard the men begin to talk about how she and Heath had known each other in high school, but she didn't hear his whole response. She tried not to drift off again into sleep as they kept moving through the quiet of the night, but her body had hit a brick wall and she was lulled into sleep as the sound of the car on the highway drowned out her thoughts.

"Eleanor."

Someone was shaking her shoulder. "Wake up, Eleanor."

Heath. It was Heath. Eleanor opened her eyes and blinked up at him. The sun was just starting to crest in the sky and she found she and Heath were the only two in the car now. His temple now sported what looked like very fresh stitches and a nasty looking purple bruise spread from either side of the wound. His bandage-wrapped arm was in a sling.

"You should be lying in a hospital bed," she said, bringing a bark of laughter from him.

"It's a scratch. No biggie."

She shook her head. Tell that to her back. It would

never forgive her for trying to carry a hardened operative on it.

"We need to get you inside. We've lost our tail and since we knocked out the tracking device they planted on you, they shouldn't be able to pick us up again, but I'd still like to get you inside."

Eleanor could see the rest of the team was standing outside the car, their backs to them. They were in front of a small roadside motel.

"Tracking device?" She shifted and slid along the seat following Heath outside the door.

"The guy who tried to grab you at the airport must have slipped it into your pocket as insurance. It was in the outside pocket of your jacket," Jangles said.

Heath looked grim. "We should have found it earlier."

No one on the team argued with him and Eleanor realized they were all looking pretty pissed off. She wondered if they were always this hard on themselves.

Her stomach growled, drawing another of those slow easy grins from Zip. The guy seemed to smile at everything. It would be annoying on some people, but on him, it worked.

"Come on. Let's get you something to eat." Heath pointed at a small restaurant across from the hotel and moved that way.

Jangles and Zip fell in behind them while Merlin and Duff peeled off and went into one of the doors on the outside of the hotel.

As they crossed the parking lot of the hotel, an orange kitten wound its way through Heath's legs before scampering off to a dumpster on the side of the lot. There were two black kittens and a gray and white striped one all eyeing the group, but hanging back as though they didn't have the guts the orange one had.

"No pets on this trip, Woof," Zip said with a laugh.

Heath grinned and shrugged in a surprisingly sheepish gesture.

"Woof?" Eleanor asked.

"It's what we call Heath," Zip said. "Woof, because he finds pets everywhere he goes. They love him. Cats, dogs, pigs. Hell, he even made friends with a camel who ended up following behind him making gaga eyes at him for half our mission one time."

Jangles made kissy sounds. "She was in looooove with our pretty boy."

Eleanor was surprised to see Heath laugh at that. In high school, when people called him pretty boy, he'd always smile on the outside but she'd seen the tightness in his face when others hadn't and knew it bothered him. He had been sensitive to people who thought he was nothing more than a dumb jock.

With these guys, his laughter was genuine. He didn't seem to mind the taunting or the label.

When they'd settled into a booth and ordered food, Eleanor looked at Jangles and Zip. She was still on edge and sitting with Heath Davis so close to her their arms were touching wasn't helping any.

"So, Jangles and Zip can't be your real names. If he's Woof because of the animals that fall for him, where did Jangles and Zip come from?"

Zip smiled and answered first. "Someday I'll show you my scar. Zips right up my leg, big and ugly."

Heath growled. "You'll keep your damned scar to yourself."

That only made Zip laugh and put his hands up in mock surrender.

Eleanor looked at Jangles.

"Name's Beau and since I can't sing worth a damn, these yahoos thought they'd call me Jangles."

Eleanor grinned at them. "And Merlin and Duff?"

They all shook their heads. "They'll have to tell you their stories," Heath said.

The server came with plates of food then and Eleanor forgot all hope of conversation as she ate. The scent of the spices and roasted meats filled her nose and made her mouth water.

She couldn't remember being this hungry in a long time. She'd ordered one meal while each of the men had ordered two entrees and a few sides. She almost wished she had too after the waiter delivered the kebaps and warm soft breads.

It was only when she finally looked up from her own meal moments later that she saw the men were eating faster than she was.

"Chew, boys. It's not meant to hit your stomach in solid form."

Heath laughed. "You're one to talk. I remember you pulling the dainty little bird act when we were in high school." He raised his voice to a falsetto. "Oh, I couldn't possibly eat more than three pieces of lettuce. I'm much too delicate and dainty for that."

Eleanor drew back her arm and elbowed him in the side. He only laughed, covering the spot with his good hand as though she'd done anything more than tickle him. She was sure she hadn't. She wanted to reach out and feel his bicep, properly tempted by what she knew would be nothing but rock-hard muscle, but she didn't dare.

Jangles looked between Heath and her. "So you two dated in high school, Heath says. Was it serious? Is he the one who got away?" Jangles angled his head as he grilled her and Eleanor wished he'd go back to his food.

She felt heat flush her cheeks and she hoped she didn't look as red as she felt. This wasn't a conversation she wanted to have. Not with anyone. Any thoughts of their dating inevitably led to thinking about how it all ended. How she'd ruined everything for the man sitting next to her.

God, she didn't want to go there.

Heath cleared his throat. "We dated for a bit in our senior year."

She didn't know if she imagined the way Heath stiffened next to her.

She didn't really want to be talking about this. She'd

always been so far out of Heath's league. He was gorgeous in school and she'd been an awkward brainiac. The truth was, when he first started hitting on her, she was sure it was going to turn out to be a big joke. That if she agreed to go outside the house with him, his friends would jump out and laugh and she'd have to face the fact he'd set her up.

Even months later when she finally did let him take her to a game and he put his arms around her and kissed her in front of all the school afterward, she still half expected him to pull back and laugh while the others joined in.

But he didn't. And neither did any of his friends, at first.

Still, for whatever reason, she didn't want these men—his team—to look at them and wonder what Heath had seen in a girl like her. So she put the attention on Heath.

"Heath was the star of our football team, even though he wasn't the quarterback. All the boys wanted to be him and all the girls wanted to have him."

"And you did," Jangles said.

Well, hell, that had backfired on her.

Eleanor looked at Heath but he was looking down at his plate now, making sure he got every last scrap of food into him. She recognized the look, though, and hated herself for putting it there.

She shouldn't have brought up his football career. To most people in their school, Heath was a happy jock, content to play ball and squeak out only the requisite grades needed to stay on the team.

When she started tutoring him in his sophomore year, she'd quickly realized he used jokes and his status as the star wide receiver to cover the fact that he was struggling in his classes. And he hated it. Hated feeling like he wasn't smart enough. Like everyone around him was better than him somehow.

She had done her best to make sure he saw that he wasn't stupid. But now, she'd just gone and brought it all back to him because she didn't want his teammates questioning her about their relationship.

She cleared her throat and this time she made damned sure she got them all the way away from their high school years.

"So, what's our plan for getting into Kazarus?"

Heath grabbed at the chance to move on and answered immediately. "They'll be expecting us to enter at one of the legal border crossings so we're not going to do that."

"You're going to smuggle me across the border?"

"Yup." This came from Zip who seemed to be entertained by her shock.

"Won't that be dangerous?" She looked to Heath but it was Jangles who answered.

"It will be, but no more dangerous than waltzing you up to a border crossing and having someone get to you with a sniper rifle or a roadside bomb."

As Eleanor's stomach seemed to hit the floor,

Heath's hand landed on her leg and he squeezed, reassuring her.

"We got you, Nori. We'll be right there with you through this."

It was stupid that she was so comforted by his use of her old nickname. She'd been Eleanor for so long now, she'd forgotten that it felt good to have friends close enough to give you a name that says you belong to them in some way. That says you're theirs or part of their group.

Not that her nickname was like the names these guys had given each other. Those were something more. Those were the mark of a band of brothers, of men who would and probably had laid their lives on the line for each other.

But hearing her old high school nickname reminded her that she'd once been more than the woman who was so driven to succeed in her job that she'd let all other parts of life—friends, family, any outside interests—fall by the wayside.

She looked at Heath. "Shouldn't you be sitting this out now? You're hurt."

He looked positively affronted and his teammates snickered. "I'm good. The bullet only grazed my arm."

"You passed out! More than once." She looked from him to the other men and back. Was she the only sane person at the table? They should be helicoptering him out of there so he could recover.

Heath shrugged. "I'll take a back seat on things for a few days, but I got a PRP and I'm good to go."

She shook her head and looked to the other men.

Jangles translated. "Platelet rich plasma injection. He'll be fine." He acted like that was the end of the discussion and went on talking about their plans for getting her and her team to the meeting. "The team that has your assistant and the rest of your group is bringing them across the border toward the west. We're heading east to circle around. We'll each come at Demir's compound from a different direction but we'll meet up a few miles outside of it and come in together for the meeting."

Heath nodded. "And while we're on the ground at the compound, we'll be with you every step of the way."

Eleanor pushed back her plate. Zip was quietly ordering food to go for Merlin and Duff.

"You said you know some of the guys on the team that's getting my people?" She asked Heath.

"Yeah. My buddy Ris is on it, but we've worked with all the guys. And Jangles went through basic with Nan."

"Nan?"

"He'll have to tell you about it," Jangles and Heath said at the same time.

Eleanor laughed and it felt good. She needed that. She didn't like the idea of heading into this negotiation without a lot of time to prep on the way with her assistant and her team. She would normally be studying information and data they fed to her and talking about all the possible scenarios and ways this could play out.

Instead, she was barely keeping her head afloat as these operatives whisked her across the country and prepped to smuggle her across the border. It brought new meaning to the term foreign service.

"So, you're married?" Zip asked and Eleanor choked on the water she'd just made the unfortunate mistake of sipping at the wrong time.

When she finished coughing, thanks in large part to Heath patting her on the back with a large hand that felt entirely too good on her body, she shook her head. "Not married."

Jangles and Zip shared a look and Zip explained. "Heath said you got married."

Eleanor turned her eyes on Heath.

His brow wrinkled. "The name change. Eleanor Bonham?"

Realization dawned and Eleanor realized she couldn't at all blame him for thinking that. In fact, if she ever ran into people she'd known in high school—which she didn't—she realized they would think the same thing.

"I took my stepfather's name," was all she said. She could feel Heath's questioning gaze on her, but she didn't say more.

She was worried about the upcoming trip and worried for her team. Yes, they'd gotten news they were safe, but they'd be starting their own roundabout trek to the meeting point.

Beth was always on top of things and didn't have any issues with pivoting when she needed to, but Marcus was probably freaking out at the changes. He could be high strung at times and wouldn't do well with things shifting on the fly. Hell, he sometimes got fidgety when a meeting was delayed or a report was late coming in.

"Did the other guys check my team for trackers? They can't find them, can they?"

Heath shook his head. "They checked. They're all clear and just like with you, they aren't giving anyone the specifics of their locations."

She nodded and pressed her lips together. She would have to trust they'd be okay.

The food for Merlin and Duff had arrived and the group stood to go back to the hotel.

Before she stepped out the door, she looked to Heath once again. The men all looked like they were on, just like they had been throughout the meal. They were always casually scanning, always checking their surroundings. Always aware of what was happening.

She lowered her voice. "Are you guys sure there was only the one tracker on me? They aren't going to find us here?"

She was worried about herself, but she was also worried about Heath and his team. She was the reason Heath was here, both in the Army and on this particular mission. He was already injured. She couldn't stand the thought that he might be hurt further. Or worse.

Heath put his good arm around her and squeezed and not for the first time, felt the guilt of all that had happened rush back to her. That and the stupid attraction she couldn't seem to fend off. Her body's response to him wasn't something she seemed to have control of. It took nothing more than a glance his way to have memories of his hands and mouth on her come rushing back, overwhelming her in the process.

She shook her head and focused on the present. The other men were flanking them and didn't seem to bat an eye at his protective gesture. Maybe he was like this with all the women they protected and it was something his team was used to seeing.

"We scanned you and your bags while you were asleep. You're clear. They won't be able to track us that way again," Jangles said.

Okay, so that should have been creepy knowing they had scanned her while she was asleep and presumably gone through her things. She should probably be angry, but she wasn't. She trusted these guys. Trusted Heath.

She took a deep breath and, with Heath still holding her tight to his side, stepped out into the night.

But as they crossed the parking lot to the hotel, Heath took a napkin out of his pocket and she saw he'd taken half of his meat and broke it up for the cats.

The guys laughed and shook their heads when Heath went and deposited the gift by the dumpsters for the hungry kittens, but Eleanor didn't laugh.

No, her heart did a little flip in her chest at that. And damn if she didn't fall a little bit in love with the big burly guy who would save his scraps for dumpster kitties.

CHAPTER 6

Heath watched Eleanor sleep from across the room. His arm was killing him and he should have taken his shift sleeping but he didn't want to leave her side yet.

Not that he didn't trust the guys on his team. These were his brothers and he knew they'd protect her with all they were, same as he would. But he was still thinking about the fact that she'd said she wasn't married.

Why did that do something to him? He had no business wanting her the way he did. Wanting to have her back in his life. But his body wasn't getting the message. He'd been half hard for her since the minute he'd set eyes on her. Didn't seem to matter that it was a completely inappropriate response.

His body recognized her and there was no talking it out of the reaction.

He thought back to what they'd had in high school.

He'd wanted a future with her back then. He had known from the minute they met that she was someone amazing. She was smart and funny and so damned sexy.

Now, he could see she was that and so much more. She'd always been book smart. It didn't surprise him one bit that she was in the position she was at with the State Department or that she was being sent on an assignment like this one. This was no little thing. Demir was known for his ability to play with the people around him and to manipulate every interaction, every engagement to his advantage.

She had to be good at what she did for them to be sending her in to lead this negotiation.

He wanted to know the rest of her story. He didn't remember her having a stepfather in high school. He wondered when he'd come into the picture and why Eleanor had decided to take his name, even though she had clearly been an adult when it happened.

He wondered everything about her. Just thinking about what had happened to her that last month they were in school made the old rage slam through his blood, seeming to boil him from the inside out. He hadn't been able to keep her safe then. He'd been so naïve, not even smart enough to realize she needed protecting. And she'd paid the price for his incompetence.

He wanted to know if she'd gotten past it. Had she been happy in life despite what happened?

He wanted to know that and so much more. What did she do when she wasn't working? Was there someone else waiting for her at home? Just because she wasn't married didn't mean there wasn't someone else.

And what was wrong with him that he wanted to go sit on the bed with her like some creeper? What the fuck was that about?

Sure, he'd thought about her some over the years. Okay, he'd thought about her a lot. More than he should. But, she'd been the first one to make him feel like he wasn't dumber than everyone around him. Somehow, she'd been able to explain things to him that brought his Ds up to Cs and even a few Bs.

It wasn't until he got into the military that anyone else saw in him what Eleanor had. That anyone else made him feel like he was smart enough to be more than a piece of muscle.

Go figure. He thought he was joining the military to be just that for them: a strong guy who could do things with his body that other people couldn't. But then he'd gotten into the Rangers and they'd taken him seriously for the first time. They'd taught him discipline and how to plan things through instead of just having fun or going off the cuff, making decisions based on emotions instead of hard cold facts and planning.

From there he'd gone to Delta where they expected him to study strategy and learn to speak other languages. He had to know how to do more than just turn a computer on. No one treated him like the jock or the class clown. Not one person there had assumed he couldn't do it. In fact, they'd been damned sure he could.

And he did.

But that had all started with the woman lying in the bed across the room.

Heath pressed his feet to the ground to keep from going over to her. Fisted his good hand into a ball to keep from closing the space between them to brush a lock of hair off her face.

His other arm ached where he'd taken a bullet and the stitches Zip had put into his temple were itchy. He'd taken a cocktail of vitamins C and A, along with some zinc, to help him heal up but his body needed time and rest. He knew that.

Still, he wasn't ready to leave her side.

Maybe if she hadn't climbed in his lap the way she had when she was trying to cover them up in that bar. His body still tightened at the thought of her, his hands aching to hold her again, to pull her flush and feel all that softness against him.

Maybe if she hadn't jumped between him and a guy who would have shot him dead without a second thought. Or if she hadn't refused to leave him when the effects of the blow to his head meant he was putting her at risk instead of saving her the way he should have been.

Then, maybe he wouldn't be feeling what he was.

Wishing for things he wasn't meant to have. Wishing for more than he could hope for.

His life was the military. His loyalty was to them. All he had become, he owed to his team and to the organization that had believed in him where no one else had.

Eleanor's face tightened and she tossed in her sleep.

Heath took a step toward her and stopped, waiting.

She stilled for a minute but then started up again, whimpering and throwing her head back and forth. She lifted her arm and cried out.

To hell with this. Heath crossed the room in three large steps, pulling his arm out of his sling and tossing it aside. He settled onto the bed with her, pulling her close to him.

"Shhhhh, it's okay Nori. I've got you."

How many times had he said that to her in the last two days? It was true, though. This time, he'd be there for her. He wouldn't let her get hurt the way he had when they were kids. He'd have her back until she was safe at home and he had to watch her walk away again. Until he had to give her up again.

Duff was taking his turn outside her door while Zip had the back of the hotel. They'd rotate soon and the others would take over. But Heath was staying right here.

Heath moved his hand over Eleanor's temple and down her cheek, soothing her back to sleep. He hated seeing her suffer. He shifted and lay on the bed, stretching out alongside her like he'd done so many years ago. A lifetime ago.

He tried to ignore the fact that she felt so damned right in his arms. Like she'd been made to be there. Or maybe it was the other way around. Like he'd been made for her.

She snuggled into him and he watched as her face evened out, the strain of the dream leaving her.

He might not have anything to offer her after this mission, but he would damn sure see that she was taken care of for as long as he was with her. However short a time that might be.

CHAPTER 7

"I need to call my boss before we hit the road," Eleanor said when they'd finished breakfast.

Heath stood before any of the others could. "I'll take you back to the room. We have a secure phone you can use."

Eleanor nodded and followed him out. This time the little orange kitten pranced up to Heath and wove between his legs. One of his little black-haired brothers followed him out and meowed loudly at Heath.

Heath went to the dumpster and knelt, placing a pile of meat on the ground for them.

"Why don't I remember this about you when we were in high school? Certainly this pied piper thing isn't new?"

He laughed. "Wasn't the pied piper snakes?"

She scrunched her nose up. "Actually now that you say that, I think it was rats."

"Rats are cute," he said.

"Ew. The point is, why don't I remember all these animals following you around?"

His eyes heated and she was mortified at how quickly her body responded to that look.

"If I'm remembering right," he said, leaning in, his mouth going tantalizingly close to the sensitive spot behind her ear, "we didn't spend a lot of time outdoors together. Bedroom, cars, those were the places we hung out."

She flushed. It was true. They'd spent a lot of their time at her house while her mom was at work at two jobs. When they did go out to other places when she finally agreed to meet his friends, it was to football games or to friends' houses. It wasn't often they went anywhere like a restaurant or anything.

"Still," she said, waving her hand dismissively in an attempt to pretend she wasn't affected by the memories of what they did in her bedroom when her mom wasn't home, "you would think I'd have seen it sometime."

"Suzanne Cassidy had those cats."

Eleanor laughed. She did remember the three cats clawing their way up Heath's clothes so they could fuss over who got to sit on his shoulder.

He shrugged. "There was Nate Benning's dog. She was always in my lap when I was there."

Eleanor froze, memory washing over her at the mention of Nate Benning.

Heath stopped walking and looked at her, his face a dull mask. "I'm sorry. I didn't think."

She shook her head. Why would he? It had all been so long ago. And when he thought of that night he probably thought of Jason Babson. But it had been Nate's house and for Eleanor, that was enough to bring not only the memories back, but the reminder that she was the reason Heath was on this dangerous mission in the first place.

There was too much between them unsaid. Too much she was afraid to say.

He opened the door to the room he and Jangles were sharing and did that thing where they checked the whole room while she waited just inside the door. When he'd cleared it, he shut the door and retrieved a satellite phone, punching in a code and handing it to her.

Eleanor took it and crossed the room, shoving aside memories and guilt and all the emotions that were swarming her with the reappearance of Heath Davis in her life.

But she needed to focus now on putting all her energy on the job ahead of her. She dialed her boss's number as Heath went to stand sentry by the door. She knew as special forces he would have TS-SCI clearance which gave him access to top secret sensitive compartmentalized information, so there was nothing she would be discussing that he couldn't hear.

It was six a.m. where they were which made it three

in the morning in London where her boss was currently meeting with the heads of several other countries, but her boss expected calls at all hours.

"Cheryl Kenney." The crisp no-nonsense way of answering the phone was standard for her boss.

"It's Eleanor."

"I got news that you're safe but no word on where you are," her boss said. "Will they be able to get you to Demir's encampment in time?"

Eleanor looked to Heath, watching his back as she spoke. It was a watch-worthy back with the way the fabric of his shirt stretched taut over bulging muscles. Her breath caught. Lord, what would it feel like to run her hands down that back as he ….

She stopped that thought before it could go further. She couldn't go there. Wouldn't.

"They assure me they can," she answered her boss.

Cheryl didn't ask where they were and Eleanor didn't offer the information. After the two attempts on her life, she had no plans to break the protocol Heath's team had set out for her, even with Cheryl. She didn't in a million years think Cheryl was the leak but she wasn't going to discuss where she was either way.

"There have been some developments on the hostage front," Cheryl said. "We've got solid information on where they're being held. The push from the deputy director is going to double now that we have solid intel."

Deputy Director Clayton Hughes was leading the

push to pull back on any talks with Onur Demir while he had American hostages. He wanted them to negotiate with the ruling party to try to cut off the pipeline of weapons to terrorist groups. Of course, that meant dealing with a government who was known for committing atrocities and human rights violations against its own people.

It wasn't an easy decision.

Eleanor focused on the intel on the hostages. "Are they at the compound?"

The hostages were going to be the trickiest part of this negotiation. There was no way around it. It would be messy and complicated and she'd be walking a tightrope where they were concerned.

"No," Cheryl answered. "They're at a nearby bunker. We're talking to the UK and France about our attempts to free them and Hughes is pushing for a joint raid on the bunker. I'll keep you posted."

"All right. We should be at the compound in a day and a half. If I don't hear from you before then, I'll let you know when we've arrived."

Eleanor ended the call and handed the phone to Heath.

And then it was just the two of them in the room with no one between them and no excuse of a phone call with her boss to put off the inevitable.

Eleanor shook her head and forced a smile. They both had to know they had to address their past together eventually. Still, she didn't know how to say she was sorry for what had happened. For the way she'd handled things. She hadn't ever thought she'd have this conversation and she'd honestly buried things so deep, she didn't know how to bring them up and into the open now.

But there was no time to say anything as Heath's team filed quietly into the room and gathered their go bags to move out.

She pushed all thoughts of their past aside. She needed to be thinking of the mission. It was too important not to. She wasn't going to be able to offer military troops to Demir and his people. The US's support of him wouldn't be anything so blatant and visible as that. But she had arms and monetary support to offer if the talks went the way they wanted them to go. First, though, she needed to get in there and feel things out with Demir. Her first job would be to assess the man and assess whether the US should put money and support behind him.

Heath came up beside her and put a hand on her lower back, warm and strong and firm. It shouldn't have done things to her the way it did. Especially not with all of his teammates in the room and all that still hung around them, but it did. Lord, she wanted to turn and sink into him, to let their bodies come together so the heat she was feeling deep in her belly could spread to all of her.

"All set?" He asked, the simple question seeming to carry so much weight.

It was just a question, she reminded herself. It wasn't him asking if she needed anything, if she was all right given all that had happened. If he could help her.

It wasn't all of that. And yet, it seemed like it was.

They hung back as the others checked the hall outside the door to the room. When Merlin ducked his head in and gave the all clear, they moved together to the SUV. And when Heath settled in next to her in the back seat, she felt safe. Despite all that had happened and all of what was to come, she felt safe.

CHAPTER 8

Heath shook Eleanor awake. He hated to do it but he had to. They were coming up on their chosen border crossing and he wanted her awake and alert for this. They'd been driving straight through, stopping only for the bare essentials for the last eight hours. They would be meeting up with her team the following day before making the final approach to Demir's compound.

She came awake slowly, blinking up at him before flushing and lifting her head off his shoulder. He cursed the loss. He'd liked having her leaning on him like that.

Come to think of it, he liked the way she looked waking up next to him, mussed and dazed.

Fuck. He shifted in his seat. He needed to stop that train of thought before he embarrassed himself in front of his team.

Eleanor wasn't making it easy. She had pulled her

hair out of the ponytail she'd had it in and was running her hands through it. Her smell drifted to him, soft and slightly sweet, tempting and teasing. He wanted to reach out and pull her to him. To bury his head in her hair and breathe her in. To lose himself in her body.

She looked out at the darkened night sky. "Where are we?"

"We're a half mile from the border to Kazarus. We're crossing over on the property of a guy we've worked with before. When we come up on his property, he'll signal us if it's okay to come onto his land. If it's clear, we'll be using a tunnel that goes from his property to his cousin's on the other side of the border. If there are patrols nearby, he'll signal us to wait."

"Patrols?" She asked.

Zip answered from the other side of her. "Shouldn't be an issue. We're just being cautious. It wouldn't really be a good thing to be caught bringing a representative of the state department into the country without clearing it with the royals."

Merlin slowed the SUV and Eleanor watched the road ahead of them.

"What will the signal look like?" She whispered the words and Heath couldn't help but laugh.

He stage-whispered back at her, "I'd tell you but I'd have to kill you," and she rewarded him with a playful elbow to the gut.

He loved when she joked with him like she used to.

When she let go with him and let down those walls she always kept around herself.

A light came on up ahead and Merlin picked up speed again. They were good to go.

Still, somehow Heath felt more anxious than he had before on a mission. He didn't have to be a genius to figure out why. It was the woman sitting between him and Zip. Having Eleanor here was messing with his head big time and he didn't like it. It didn't help that his injury meant he had to let his team step up and take on most of the protection detail for at least the next couple of days.

They needed to get her through this mission and home safe. The idea of it lanced through him, even as he knew it was what he wanted. He wanted her safe but that meant having her far away from here. Far away from him.

They pulled onto the farm of their host, Aksan, and toward the barn that housed the mama sheep and their babies when Aksan wanted to separate them from the rest of the flock. It also housed the tunnel.

Aksan waved them into the space and they all piled out of the SUV while Merlin paid for Aksan's trouble in American dollars. A lot of them.

The sheep and lambs began to bleat at them and Zip tipped a head toward the side of the aisle that held most of them. "Take care of that will you, Woof?"

Heath laughed, but crossed to the sheep, letting the lambs nuzzle at his good arm as they waited. They did get quieter and he saw Eleanor grinning at him and shaking her head.

Then Aksan signaled his men to lift an enormous trap door in the center aisle of the barn. The ground beneath the floor had been hollowed out into a steep ramp and Merlin steered their SUV down the slope to the bottom of the space.

The precarious slant of the car would make most people nervous but Eleanor didn't seem to bat an eye at it. Nor did she question it when she was handed a pair of night vision goggles and they all had to clamber past the car and head into a tunnel that was small enough they had to crouch and walk single file to fit.

Heath hoped like hell she continued on without issue for the mile-long trek underground. It was different than being in a tunnel in your car. One built by engineers and shored up with concrete and metal. This was nothing more than rock and dirt and without his training, it would be easy to let panic kick in at the idea that the whole thing could collapse and bury them alive.

"How we doing up there, Eleanor?" Heath asked, pitching his voice low. They didn't have to completely silent since they were only crossing under the open grazing land of Aksan's farm at the moment, but he wasn't exactly going to shout to her.

"Oh, just dandy." There was a small squeak to her voice that said she was fighting the very fear he'd just wondered about. "And you?" she asked.

He chuckled. "Hanging in. We've made this trip before. One foot in front of the other. Piece of cake."

"Piece of cake, huh?"

Jangles chimed in from in front of Eleanor. "Now would be a bad time to let us know you're claustrophobic."

"You never asked," Eleanor said and Heath didn't miss the tremble in her voice. "And besides, I didn't think I was until now."

Heath slung the strap of his weapon around to hang on his back and reached out to rest a hand on Eleanor's side, squeezing as they continued through the tunnel. At the pace they were moving at, they had a good twenty to thirty minutes to go. They needed to keep her calm through this.

"Remember that cave in the Philippines?" Zip chimed in.

Jangles groaned. "No, I don't. In fact I do my damned best not to remember those caves. Ever."

"What happened?" Eleanor asked.

"We had a little down time in the Philippines so Zip schedules this caving expedition," Heath said, ignoring how damned good it felt to have his hand on Eleanor as they moved in the dark. "Only he decides to go with this discount tour operator because, as he put it, we know what we're doing so what does it matter if our tour guide does?"

"Oh no," Eleanor said.

"Oh yes." Heath laughed at the memory. "The guy

got stuck head down in a crevice. He was wedged so deep it took us three hours to get him out of there."

"Probably not the best story for the moment," Duff said from behind them.

"I'm okay with it," Eleanor assured him and Heath could hear the strain had left her voice. She was handling this and he had so much damned pride for her. She'd been incredible through all of this. "You guys got him out?"

"We did," Jangles said. "Made for a lovely vacation."

Zip snorted. "There's no other way you'd rather spend your off time."

It was true, Heath thought. They had all loved the challenge. A body isn't made to be upside down for so long, so the guy had been in real danger. It had been a race against the clock to get him free using only what they had in their packs. They'd had to chisel a pulley system into the walls of the cave and ease him out inch by inch with ropes.

"Aksan and his cousin have a lot of people going through this tunnel?" She asked.

"Not so many that they get caught. They charge enough for it to pay off any patrols that do come by, but they keep the traffic light. They make it cost prohibitive to keep it that way," Merlin said.

"So Uncle Sam is paying a fortune to get me to Kazarus?"

Heath and the others laughed and Heath answered. "Discretionary Mission Funding."

There was laughter in her voice when she answered. "That sounds good and vague."

"Perfect. That's the way it's supposed to sound," said Zip.

Ahead of them Merlin signaled for silence and they all went quiet as they continued the trek through the dark.

As they moved through the space, Heath kept his eyes trained on Eleanor and cursed himself six ways from Sunday. He was going to hell.

Because as they snuck through a dark tunnel under the border of two nation states, he was thinking about her body. He was thinking about how soft she felt under his hand. He was thinking about how good her silhouette looked even through his night vision goggles and how much he wished they were alone in the dark, and not in a tunnel.

Yeah, he was going to hell. He grinned. Might as well sit back and enjoy the trip.

CHAPTER 9

Eleanor didn't realize how worried she was about her team until she saw them all waiting by their vehicle at the rendezvous point two miles out from Demir's compound. They stood by their vehicle on the side of a road surrounded by rocky outcroppings and shrubs. White, blue, and yellow wildflowers dotted the landscape and if she wasn't feeling on edge, she would be happy for the chance to take in the view.

She hoped they wouldn't be there long. She felt exposed.

"You're all okay?" She asked for the third time.

This time, her assistant Beth laughed at her, as did the other three people going into the negotiations with them.

"We had a gorgeous drive down the coast. It was beautiful," Beth gushed.

Eleanor forced a smile. She'd seen the coastline of

Turkey before and knew how breathtaking it was. She'd been surprised on her first trip here. She had thought Turkey would be sandy, all deserts and dunes. There were rock faces but they were beautiful and filled in with lush green shrubs and trees.

Her team had come down the western coast so they'd had the treat of ocean views and coastal breezes for their trip.

Beth had been her assistant since the woman graduated from college six years earlier. She had moved up through two promotions with Eleanor and they worked well together. She was uber organized and usually able to predict what Eleanor needed, even if she did have an addiction to romance novels Eleanor just couldn't understand.

Eleanor had worked with Geoff, Sharon, and Marcus all before and liked them, for the most part. They had all worked to get where they were and didn't seem to feel entitled to their positions. Her boss had let her choose who was coming on the trip with her and it had been a no-brainer to choose this team.

Geoff and Sharon had a lot of experience and she respected their opinions. That was important going into something like this.

Marcus, the youngest of the group, took a step closer to her. "It's good to see you here in one piece. They wouldn't tell us anything about where you were."

Eleanor nodded. It was meant to be that way, with no one on her team or from her office knowing exactly where she was. She hated the fact that this whole thing had put her in doubt of the people standing around her right now. She needed to trust them to do her job. Needed to know they had her back as she went into these talks.

She raised her gaze to the man she knew she could trust above all others. Heath stood talking to two of five men who had escorted her team to the meetup, but his eyes were on her as he spoke. Her and the area around them, she realized. He was watching, always careful not to let his guard down.

She was grateful for that.

He crossed to her and introduced her to the two men who followed. "Eleanor, this is Ris and Nan. They've been with your team the last couple days." He turned to the men. "This is Nor—uh, Eleanor."

Eleanor flushed at his almost use of her old nickname. If she were really being honest with herself, she would admit that she'd missed the way her name sounded coming from him. Even when he said it here in front of other people, it made her heart race the way it had when he'd first told her he liked her after a tutoring session when they were teens.

Of course, back then, she'd thought he might be teasing her or setting her up for some horrible joke where the rest of the football team would jump out of hiding to make fun of her.

But things were different between them now.

So much of what had happened back then shaped

who they were today. Hell, if it all hadn't happened the way it had, he would have gone to a college near her school and played ball while she pursued her degree. He wouldn't have ended up enlisting straight out of high school. He wouldn't be here trying to sneak her into a dangerous negotiation that could go wrong at any turn.

She plastered a smile on her face and shook hands with the burly men in front of her. "Nan, Ris, thanks for being part of this. We appreciate all you're doing to make this negotiation happen."

The men grinned and Ris gave her one of those drawling, "Just doing our jobs, ma'am," lines. Somehow, his flirting managed to not be offensive.

At least not to her. Heath was giving Ris a glare that could scare the pants off a four-star general. He was all muscle and chiseled features. He looked like a comic book super hero come to life.

And she had to laugh when Ris winked at Heath. She couldn't believe how much these guys all ribbed each other during their missions.

Heath stepped between her and the other men, taking her by the elbow. Luckily for him, his grip was gentle, not controlling, or he'd be getting a mouthful and then some from her. As it was, she had to tell herself not to read too much into his actions.

"You're going to ride with me. We're heading to the hotel first and then we'll go to the compound."

They walked to the SUV that her team had arrived

in and she, Heath, Beth, Zip, and Duff loaded in. Duff took the wheel. She looked behind them to see the others all loading into the other vehicle with Merlin driving that one and Jangles sitting in the back. She wondered how Ris and Nan's team was going to get to wherever their next assignment was but no one seemed to be concerned about it.

She shook her head. Special forces. Knowing them, they'd just walk off into the woods somewhere and melt into the landscape until someone needed them.

Heath took the spot to the right of her and Beth and Zip sat behind them.

Heath leaned in. "Coming and going from the compound each day will be our most vulnerable times. When we load up each day, I want you to listen and follow directions. Don't question anything the team or I tell you to do. Just do it. I'll be right next to you when we come and go and we'll be on alert."

She nodded and he continued.

"Same goes for the hotel. Listen to what the team tells you to do. We won't be ordering room service or anything like that. We have two teams here, so we'll have our guys get food and bring it in. If you wake up and you're restless, there's no going out for a walk or going down to the fitness center or anything like that. You'll stay in the hotel room at all times unless one of us tells you to leave."

She bit down on her lips to keep from smiling. It wasn't funny. What he was telling her wasn't at all entertaining and her reaction wasn't at all like her. She was professional. Always. She was the one who kept her head together during stressful times and always had a plan that was two steps ahead of those around her.

So why was she falling apart right now? This was her life and possibly the lives of her team on the line. Still, she couldn't help it. He was sexy when he was being bossy and for some reason, that made her want to laugh.

He leaned in even closer and growled. "Are you laughing at me, Nori?"

She shook her head. "Not even a little," she tried, but the choked way the words came out completely belied the statement.

And damn, now she was truly laughing and she didn't know why. She waved a hand at him as her eyes started to water with the effort of holding back the laughter. "It's nerves," she said, but then she lost it and she was full out laughing as he glowered at her.

Jesus, this didn't happen to her. She didn't fall apart. Not ever. She held herself together through everything that could possibly happen in her work.

Beth was joining in on it in the back seat and Zip was smiling as he watched Heath growl at her while she and Beth lost it.

Eleanor wiped at her eyes and got herself under control. "Sorry, it's not funny. It's just been a long few days."

She and Beth managed to hold it together for a few seconds and Eleanor thought maybe she'd salvage her reputation as one of the top negotiators for the United States.

Then Beth piped up from the backseat. "Like an alpha male," and Eleanor knew she was talking about the romance novels she was always reading.

Heath shot Beth a look complete with growl and Eleanor laughed again.

It was all over.

CHAPTER 10

Two hours later, Eleanor was finally doing the work she should have been doing this whole time with her team.

While Zip and Duff stood guard in the corners of the hotel room, they were poring over every last detail the government had about Onur Demir and his rebels. Heath was watching from a nearby chair but he was officially off duty and supposedly resting. He didn't look like he was resting to her. He'd taken off his sling but refused to leave the room, and she had a feeling telling him to go lie down wouldn't have any affect so she didn't try. She didn't believe in wasted energy on lost causes.

She also noticed he was being particularly testy with the male members of her team. He'd actually growled at Geoff at one point when Geoff tried to hold the door for her.

She shook her head and focused on Demir instead. He wasn't what you'd expect in a rebel leader. He came from a family who was nearly as wealthy and well connected as the monarchy in Kazarus. He'd grown up with wealth and privilege. But somewhere along the way, he'd developed the notion that the people of Kazarus should be able to live a free life under democratic rule.

Beth summarized what they knew. "His family is wealthy and was once powerful, though they've lost some of that power in recent decades. His grandfather was a general in the country's military before the current regime took over. He died during the coup and Demir's father barely escaped with his life. He and his younger brother, Farid, both fight in the Kazarus Freedom Army. Onur as its founder and head, and Farid as his right-hand man."

Marcus picked up the narrative. "Onur was educated in Turkey and the US before coming home to Kazarus to establish the KFA. It started out as a small group of protesters but it quickly grew and estimates suggest he has an army of over ten thousand men. There are up to fifty thousand civilians forming a network of support across the nation."

With a population of only 1.5 million people in the small nation, those were not insignificant numbers.

"So far, they've kept their attacks to military installations and government offices," Geoff added.

"So far?" Eleanor asked. "Do we think that's going to change?"

Her team looked distinctly uncomfortable.

Geoff offered an answer first. "It's hard to say. When the group first formed, they funded their efforts by kidnapping people from wealthy Kazarus families, but they were careful not to extend those efforts to visitors from other nations. It's said Demir believed the fight should be kept within Kazarus, not only its borders, but among only its people."

Marcus took up the explanation. "On the whole, they no longer do that. They're well-funded now and they're striving for greater legitimacy. But they've broken with this new stance recently when they kidnapped several nurses and doctors that were here delivering free surgical care as part of a charity from the US, UK, and France. We don't know what that means."

"Or what his intentions are with them," Geoff said. "He's made no demands so far."

"He's had them for two months now?" Eleanor asked, although she knew she was right. She'd already been through the file. She was mostly trying to talk through all they knew so that her thoughts could begin to gel where Onur Demir is concerned.

Her team all nodded in response.

"That's the unknown in all of this," she said. "I don't like it. Did Cheryl send any other intel on where they're being held?"

"Not much," Beth said, pulling out a sheet of paper and handing it to Eleanor. "It's an underground bunker left over from the tail end of World War I when the country was part of the Ottoman Empire just before its fall. When Kazarus reestablished its independence during the Arab Revolt, the ruling party of the time—the now defunct Kazarus Arab Military—took over the bunker. Kazarus lost its freedom again briefly just before World War II when it was occupied by Iraq."

"We think at some point after the second world war," Marcus said, "when Kazarus took back its independence and the current monarchy was established, the bunker was abandoned. It's not clear whether anyone was using it between then and whenever Demir chose to use it. Our guys haven't gotten eyes in there yet to see what the underground portion is like or what condition it's in now."

Eleanor looked at her watch. It wasn't very late, but she was worn out from the last few days. As much as she'd like to keep poring over what they had, she knew it was just as important to go in there tomorrow rested and sharp. If she was off her game at all, she could very well mess this up.

Tomorrow, she would need to assess whether Onur Demir was an ally the US wanted to foster or one they should cut loose before they formed the kind of potentially messy entanglement they were considering. She could look at the intel they had for days, but when it came right down to it, meeting this guy and getting a hands-on feel for what he was capable of was what would get the job done for her boss.

She stood. "Okay guys, let's get some rest. We need to check in with Cheryl in the morning before we head out to see if she has any further information for us. Let's meet back here at oh-five-hundred."

To their credit, none of them groaned at the hour she quoted. They stood and filed out of the room. Duff gave Heath and her a silent nod before following her team.

Their group had taken over the entire floor of the hotel. She'd be staying in this room with her team across the hall in two of the rooms on that side of the hotel with the Deltas in rooms surrounding them.

Eleanor wondered if Heath would be staying with her overnight again. She felt better waking with his arms around her the other night. She woke from a nightmare where this time, she hadn't been able to shake off the man who tried to grab her at the airport. She'd seen Heath running for her but it was too late as the man pulled her into a van and the van drove away as she struggled helplessly against his strength.

But Heath had been there when she woke and had held her as she'd drifted back to sleep, something she knew she wouldn't have been able to do if he hadn't been there holding her.

She turned to him now to find him picking up her small suitcase and shoulder bag.

"Come on," he said, tilting his head toward the

LORI RYAN

dividing door between her room and the room next to it.

"Where are we going?" She followed even as she asked the question.

He opened the door and Zip was there on the other side, holding that side open.

"We're moving you to another room. We'll bring you back here in the morning, but in the meantime, the room everyone thinks you're in is going to be empty," Heath said as Zip closed and locked the dividing door.

Duff opened the door that led to the hallway and silently waved them forward. Heath put a finger to his lips to tell her to be quiet and then slipped out the door with her bags in that stealth way they had of moving without making a sound.

She followed with what she hoped were quiet enough steps as they slipped out and turned right down the hallway. He went to the second door from the end on the left-hand side of the hall and it opened from the inside.

Jangles stood sentry inside, holding the door for them before slipping out himself with a grin and tap of his fingers to his temple for her.

"Flirt," Heath groused as he put her suitcase on the bed.

Eleanor shook her head but she couldn't help but smile. "He's just being nice, Heath."

He only shook his head and she knew she wouldn't win that argument.

"Heath, I—" she paused. She wanted to say something about what had happened between them when they'd last seen each other years before. About how they'd left it all. She needed to clear the air.

"No." The word came from him, husky and thick as he turned to face her.

He wasn't touching her, wasn't even near her, but there was tension thick and heady in the air between them.

"No, we shouldn't talk?" She managed to get out.

"No need. The past is the past. I have a job to do now and so do you."

She watched him and finally gave a nod. Heath was stubborn. Always had been. If he wasn't going to let her talk to him about their past, she would have to wait until he was ready.

She moved to her suitcase and began to fidget, looking through it for the things she would need to get ready for bed. Would he leave and sleep in one of the other rooms for the night? She didn't need to have a guard on her at all times, but God she wanted it.

She didn't want to let him know how shook up she felt from the attempt to grab her at the airport. Her hand slipped and her toothpaste fell to the floor.

Heath was there, picking it up and handing it to her. The move brought him close again and he stood, inches from her for a minute. He was watching her mouth and she knew if she leaned in on tiptoe, he would close his mouth over hers and kiss her the way he used to.

Only she knew it would be nothing like it used to be. He wasn't the young kid he was when they were together before.

Everything about this man said he knew what he was doing in the bedroom. He was intense and in control. He was no mere boy now. He had the experience of the world behind him and Eleanor had a feeling that experience would tell him how to touch her. How to kiss her and tease her and bring her to the point of begging before letting her orgasm in his arms.

She shook her head and stepped back, wanting to step forward instead. Wanting for all the world to lose herself in this man's arms.

Her action seemed to break the spell that hung between them and he moved away.

"I'll wait outside while you get yourself ready. Call for me when you're done."

Eleanor nodded and picked up her toiletries and her night clothes.

She would shower and dress and wash the cobwebs from her brain. It was all too clear that she wasn't thinking the least bit clearly. And that would be dangerous going into a job like this.

CHAPTER 11

Heath watched Eleanor sleep, knowing she needed to be well rested today. For that matter, so did he. He needed to be sharp to make sure nothing happened to Eleanor, but somehow he'd been nothing but off kilter since the start of this assignment.

He'd been dozing in the armchair in her room, but the pain in his arm had woken him at three in the morning and he hadn't gone back to sleep again.

She looked so beautiful sleeping. When they were dating back in high school, they'd never spent the night together. They had stolen moments at her house when her mom was at work or in the back of his Mustang parked on Hillman's Pass at the top of the overlook where all the high school kids went to make out. But he'd never been able to fall asleep with her and wake up with her in the morning.

Not that this was really sleeping together, him in a

chair and her on the bed. He wanted to curl up in the bed with her and pull her to him, but that wasn't a smart move. He couldn't continue to be stupid where this woman was concerned.

He wasn't one of those people who fantasized about what couldn't be. Not since he was a kid when he'd thought he could somehow earn his dad's approval if he just tried hard enough to be the son his dad wanted. There was no making yourself into something you weren't.

She mumbled something incoherent and rolled in her sleep, snuggling deeper under the covers.

Closing his eyes, he ran through all the scenarios for the morning. All the plans in place for getting her in and out of the compound safely. That was where they would be most at risk, on the way to and from the negotiations.

The compound itself should be fairly safe from attack. Demir and his men kept it fortified and guarded from any outside attack by the Kazarus military.

Unless an attack came from the inside.

Heath's job was to think of any and all possibilities, to know where an attack would come from before it did.

So why did this feel more like him panicking over what could happen to Eleanor than him being prepared?

"You're not sleeping," Eleanor said sleepily, pulling him from his thoughts.

He shushed her, not wanting to disturb her sleep. "It's all right. I was just thinking."

"Can't sleep?" She asked, shifting again so the sheet shifted, revealing one long lean leg to the thigh.

Hell, she was going to kill him. She needed her sleep. He should get up and leave and take his insomnia somewhere else.

"Heath, I want to say something and I want you to listen to me and not try to stop me, okay?"

He fought not to freeze at her words. "Okay."

She didn't look at him when she spoke, keeping her eyes focused somewhere over his shoulder.

"I want to say I'm sorry, Heath. For so much, but mostly for hiding that night, for getting you into trouble with your dad."

Now Heath did freeze. What the hell was she talking about?

"Sorry?" He tried not to let the words come out as a growl, but it wasn't easy. "What the hell do you think you have to apologize for?"

Her eyes found his but then dropped just as quickly as she looked away from him.

"If I hadn't hidden after …" he saw her swallow, "after it happened, you wouldn't have been picked up by the cops. And if I'd just talked to you after that, maybe you wouldn't have gone after Jason. Your dad wouldn't have forced you out. You wouldn't have had to join the Army. All of it. I'm just… I'm just really sorry it all happened."

Heath's head swam. He couldn't say he wasn't sorry it had all happened. The night his football teammate—a guy he thought was his friend and a good person—attacked Eleanor, coming pretty damned close to raping her, had been a nightmare he would never wish on her or any other woman.

He hated that he wasn't there to stop it. Hated it had been because of him that it happened. But he'd never once blamed her for any of it.

He moved to the bed and sat, then cupped her face, bringing his eyes to hers. "I know you're smart enough to know what Jason did wasn't your fault."

Her eyes flashed. "I know that."

"Then why would you think my dad kicking me out was your fault? Eleanor, my dad and I were fighting all the time and me being in trouble was nothing new."

She shook her head. "That's not true. When we were dating, you had stayed out of trouble. You guys were getting along better."

He snorted. "I was staying out of trouble, but he and I weren't getting along. And yeah, that last week there before graduation was bad, but I'd long ago pushed him to the brink of patience with me."

He and his dad had never gotten along. His dad had been ready to kick him out for a long time. When Jason assaulted Eleanor, Heath had been outside with friends doing keg stands. The only thing that saved her from rape was the police raiding the party at that moment.

Heath's friends had all run when the cops arrived,

but Heath knew Eleanor had gone upstairs to fix her hair. He wasn't going to run off and leave her just to avoid getting into trouble with his dad. So he'd gone looking for her and the police had caught him, but that was on him, not on her. None of it had been on her.

"Nori, I don't blame you at all for hiding that night. Hell—" it was his turn to look away now— "I should have been there with you instead of partying downstairs. I should have gone with you that night. I should have seen that Jason was a piece of shit so pissed off you were taking my attention away from the team and the guys. That he was the kind of guy that would stoop to rape to break us apart."

She was shaking her head. "It wasn't your fault."

He leaned closer, touching his forehead to hers and bringing his hand to her cheek. He wanted to be closer, but this was as good as it was going to get right now. "None of that was your fault either. It was Jason's fault. He was the one who was wrong here. And as for my dad kicking me out of the house, it wasn't a bad thing."

Eleanor hadn't answered his calls or come to the door when he went to her house after that night and he'd had no idea why. She wouldn't see him. But a few days later, he'd finally gotten it out of one of the other guys what Jason had done. And he'd lost it. He'd never been in such a blind rage before.

When he put Jason in the hospital, the school suspended Heath. Only his dad's money had kept it a suspension instead of expulsion. He was allowed to graduate from high school, but not allowed to walk with the class and his dad had told him he wasn't paying another penny for Heath.

That had included college. So he'd joined the Army. And that was the best thing to happen to him.

Well, the best thing if he didn't count Eleanor. She'd been, hands down, the best part of his life. It had all gone to hell and ended in the worst way possible, but for those months they'd been together, it was perfection.

He couldn't believe she'd been thinking there was anything she needed to apologize for. "Joining the Army was the right thing for me. Much better than college would have been."

She was watching him intently. "You've made it really far. I'm proud of you, Heath."

Jesus Christ, if that didn't do all kinds of things in his chest. He knew he was heading into the very dangerous territory of wanting more with Nori than just a shared past. A whole lot more.

CHAPTER 12

"No." Eleanor didn't even hesitate in her response.

Heath pushed the Abaya and Hijab at Eleanor again, this time adding a growl. She needed to wear the loose-fitting dress and head covering so he could disguise her more easily as they left the hotel.

He'd let her have her early morning meeting with her team but now he needed to separate her from the group so anyone intending to harm her wouldn't realize she wasn't in the main caravan heading to the compound.

"Yes, Eleanor. I need you covered while I get you to the negotiations."

She crossed her arms and leveled him with a look. "Absolutely not. Demir and his people are Arab Christians, not Muslims. If I show up to the negotiations dressed in that, I look like I don't know who I'm dealing with and what I'm doing. I'll look like an amateur who assumes because I'm in a Middle Eastern country, I'm expected to wear that by default. I won't weaken myself at the start of this by going in there like that."

He growled again. Damn, he was really making a habit of that. "I don't care if you take it off when we make it to the compound, but you need to put it on now."

"Not happening."

He looked at her. She had her hair pulled back in a tight knot at the nape of her neck and wore trim khaki pants and a white buttoned-down shirt with a leather belt. She had on ankle boots that, thankfully, weren't for fashion. They were laced up and functional, ready for her to run if she needed to. He loved her for all of that.

But what he didn't love was that she wouldn't let him do his job.

He moved in close, towering over her and not caring one damned bit that he was using his size to intimidate her. If it meant keeping her safe, he'd do it. "When we step foot onto that compound, you can be in charge—" at least so far as the negotiations were concerned, he added to himself, "but my job is to get you there safely. If I tell you to put this on, you'll put it on. If I tell you to get down, you'll get down. If I tell you to run, you'll run. Got it? That's the way this works, Eleanor."

Her eyes said no. They were, in fact, impressively

murderous at the moment. "I'll wear it out of the hotel and halfway to the compound, but then it's coming off. I won't have any of Demir's people see me wearing the wrong damned clothes."

He slid his jaw back and forth, trying to crack the tension he felt. "Fine."

He shoved the dark fabric at her and stepped back, watching as she donned the Abaya and expertly wrapped the Hijab like she'd done it dozens of times before.

She caught him looking as she tucked it into place. "I've worn them before. It's not the clothes I object to, Heath. And I respect you have to do your job, but I have to do mine. That means walking into this negotiation from a place of strength. Making sure Demir respects me. If I look like I don't know what I'm doing, we might as well go home right now."

He wanted to take her home. He'd been all in favor of letting her complete this mission and then getting her home safely, but today, he was all about getting her out of here. If it were up to him, he'd scoop her up and run like hell for home.

And then what? Then he'd never see her again. She'd go her way and he'd go his and she'd be out of his life again.

He rubbed at his chest. The thought gave him heartburn. At least, he'd tell himself that's what it was. Because anything else, like the fact he was falling for this woman, was too fucking much for him to handle right now.

A knock on the door told them it was time. They'd be moving her down to a car without her people and leaving ahead of the others. He and Zip were going with her. The others would take her people over.

Heath opened the door and he and Zip ushered Eleanor out and into the stairwell where Merlin and Duff had cleared the way and were standing sentry.

They moved with practiced precision and were down in the parking garage in minutes and then Zip was behind the wheel and Eleanor and Heath were in the back as they pulled out.

Heath welcomed the steely calm that came over him when he was in his element. He'd spent the night worrying about this move, worrying that he couldn't keep Eleanor safe. But now that they were under way, training and instinct took over as he scanned the area around them as they moved out into traffic.

Eleanor turned in her seat, looking behind them. "Where is my team? Where are the others?"

"Not coming," Heath said, not moving his eyes to her. "They'll come in half an hour with the rest of my team."

"What?"

He had expected the anger in her tone. He knew without asking that she'd disapprove of being split from her team. Still, no one was gunning for her team.

"Eleanor, our job is to keep you safe. This is how we make sure that happens."

She turned now, leaning toward him so he had no choice but to look her way.

"By making my team decoys? You're sticking them out there, but hiding me away?"

He shot her a look. "We're not making them decoys. They'll go out a different way. No one's going out there in the open as a target. We're going to keep all of you safe. I promise."

He looked back to their surroundings, checking for anything suspicious. "Look, Eleanor, we have a job to do and we're going to do it. Thanks to someone in your office or on your team, people knew you were coming here for what's supposed to be a black op. I'm not about to let you travel with the team now. I'm not going to let them know when and where you'll be."

He looked back her way and saw her pale.

"You moved me to another room last night because my team knew what room I was supposed to sleep in?"

"Yeah," he said, not expanding on that. He knew she wouldn't believe one of them could be the person who was leaking her whereabouts and her mission for this trip.

She'd never want to think one of them could be guilty of betraying her on such a heinous level.

But he had to believe that. He and his team anticipated the worst before it got them killed.

And in this case, before it got *her* killed.

CHAPTER 13

Eleanor was more than happy with where things had gone during the morning's talks. They were sitting down to eat now, which in theory wasn't meant to be part of the negotiations, but this was as much a part of it for her as her one-on-one talks with Demir.

She needed to see more of his people and his organization.

She saw her Delta team, as she'd come to think of them, spread out around the perimeter of the large dining room they'd just entered. They hadn't admitted to her that they were Delta but she'd checked with her boss on a last-minute call before the meeting this morning and she confirmed it.

Heath and his team were good at being present but slipping into the background when needed.

Not that Heath was ever really part of the background for her. She was aware of his presence in a way she wasn't with the others on the team. She'd seen him shadowing her throughout the compound, always within shouting distance as they moved. He wasn't wearing his sling today and the bandage on his arm was covered by a long-sleeved shirt. The stitches on his temple only served to make him look all the more threatening and scary.

Now, he took up a position not far from her and stood guard as she and Onur walked side-by-side.

The building they were in was the largest on the compound and could easily be considered a mansion with its size. There were large columns in many of the rooms, including this one, and beautiful tile mosaics. She was particularly fond of the carved wood doors and the courtyard with tiled fountain.

Eleanor knew from their research that the land and home had been in his family for several generations, but he'd built the rest of the buildings around this one in the last few years for his army. What had once been the family estate was now a paramilitary compound of sorts.

"Ms. Bonham, may I introduce my brother, Farid?" Onur raised a hand, drawing his younger brother over. No one could mistake the men for strangers. They both had dark looks and nearly matching eyes.

But there was something about Onur that Farid didn't possess. Onur Demir had a smoothness to him. A refined presence and charisma that would allow him entry into circles she would guess Farid would struggle in.

Farid had a scar that ran from his temple to the corner of his mouth. He came forward and greeted her politely, bowing his head in acknowledgment rather than shaking her hand.

She nodded her head back. "It's a pleasure."

She and her team were introduced to the others, all leaders in Demir's army. She was surprised to see many women at the top of his hierarchy, all of whom looked like they could give her Deltas a run for their money.

She smiled as she thought of the Deltas as *hers* again. She wondered what the men would think of that.

As she kept up with the conversation around her, she went through the things she wanted to cover when she and Demir were back in private talks.

One of the things she wanted to assess was how Demir viewed Christian-Muslim relations. Under the current regime, Christians were often persecuted or at the very least discriminated against. She wanted to know if he would return that persecution ten-fold to the Muslims he and his followers would share this country with, or would he allow freedom of religion for all Kazarus citizens.

So far, she hadn't spotted any Muslims in his camp, but that didn't mean he was intolerant of them. And she certainly hadn't met the entirety of his followers.

It wasn't something her government needed to

know, but she wanted the information as part of her personal assessment of where the negotiation was going. It would also help her get a sense of who he was and whether he could be trusted.

For the most part, Demir was as she'd expected. He was passionate about his cause and willing to do whatever it took to defeat the current regime in Kazarus. He was enigmatic and charming, which made sense given the number of people willing to follow him.

She had the feeling, though, that he was willing to be cruel to make sure he succeeded in his cause.

And there was something else under the surface, too. Something she wasn't able to identify. Maybe it was a sense he was holding something back. She wasn't sure, though. She needed more time with him.

"You are quiet, Ms. Bonham," Demir said, leaning in. "Is the food to your liking?"

Eleanor nodded, covering her hand with her mouth as she finished chewing and swallowed. The rich sauces and tender meats were aromatic and delicious. "It's wonderful. So much so that I'm forgetting my manners and ignoring you all for the food."

Not true. She'd been too deep in thought.

Demir smiled and lifted a bowl with torn pieces of flat bread in it, holding it out to her. "My aunt is Lebanese. You must try her Man'ouche."

Eleanor smiled as she took the offered bread and made a note of the fact his aunt was here in the compound with him.

Eleanor glanced at Demir's brother. "Family is important to you."

It was a statement but he treated it as a question and responded. "It is. Family is everything." He placed the bread bowl back on the table and turned to her, his gaze intense. "The king—to him, family is nothing more than his bloodline, that which gives him what he considers his right to claim the throne. This is wrong. It is not as it should be. Family must be above all. They are your blood, your heart, and your soul."

Eleanor nodded, hiding the pain she felt at his words. Her family was gone. Though she still had her stepfather and his wife and children in her life, her mother was gone. Her dad was gone. She had no grandparents alive on either side.

As she ate, she found herself envying what Demir had with his family. It was unlikely she'd ever have a family of her own again. It wasn't like she was going to find a man and fall in love. Not with the way she was so focused on her career. She just didn't have the bandwidth for something serious.

Her thoughts flew immediately to Heath but she shoved the idea aside. He didn't have room for a woman in his life either. That was clear.

A woman approached from Demir's other side and spoke to his brother quietly. Eleanor saw his brother lean in to speak to Demir, but she was still surprised by Demir's words when he turned to her.

"I am afraid I must cut today's session short. I have

something to see to that requires my urgent attention. We'll resume in the morning."

He wasn't asking her if that was okay, but still, she chose to answer as though he had.

"That will work for us." She gave a nod and smiled, though on the inside, she was wondering what had happened to cause the sudden cancellation.

It was definitely unusual for someone to interrupt talks of this nature and the move made her question where the talks were going.

She saw Heath step toward her and knew he must have noticed the exchange. She gave a minuscule shake of her head as she and Demir stood. Her team knew better than to react publicly to any move by someone they were negotiating with so she knew they would take it in stride. Still, she would want their take on this when they got out of here.

Heath had moved in behind her and she turned to him. "We'll be heading back to the hotel for the afternoon and evening. Can you please make any necessary arrangements with your team?"

He gave a nod and stepped to the side, talking into his comms.

"Mr. Demir, we'll see you in the morning, then?"

He gave a nod and then he was gone, his brother and two of the people she knew to be close advisors of his behind him. Two members of his security staff approached.

"We'll show you and your team out," one of them said with no expression in his face or tone.

When they were loaded into the SUVs—this time with Heath and her leaving with the rest of the convoy since they didn't have much choice in the matter— Heath was the first to ask.

"What the hell was that about?" He was looking at Merlin, who was driving the car.

"No idea," Merlin said, "but I've sent Duff to tail him and see where he goes."

"Any word of an attack or something we need to be aware of?" Eleanor asked, hoping if there was, that Heath's people would know about it.

"Nothing we've heard anything about," Merlin said as Heath pressed his leg closer to her and she wondered if the gesture was a subtle attempt to offer support.

She was glad he was circumspect. She appreciated that he respected the boundaries her career demanded. It was one thing if he didn't care if his team knew, but her people didn't need to know this was her high school boyfriend.

Eleanor looked to Beth in the third-row seat with Jangles.

Beth looked up from the tablet she'd been tapping on. "No news on our end. No one seems to know of anything that would cause him to put a halt to the talks."

"Let's not go spreading that rumor," Eleanor said.

"He didn't truly put a halt to them. They're going to continue in the morning."

Beth flushed. "I didn't mean...sorry," she mumbled.

Eleanor waved off the woman's worry. "Let's just be careful how we talk about this. I'll call Cheryl when we get to the hotel and see if she's heard anything. Then we can rest before tomorrow and make sure this gets back on track in the morning."

Heath pressed his leg to hers again and even though he was looking out the windows, scanning their surroundings, she had a feeling he'd done it on purpose.

Eleanor buried a smile. She didn't want to admit, even to herself, how good it felt to have this man beside her again.

CHAPTER 14

Eleanor was glad to see Demir at the talks the following morning. Part of her had wondered if he might have decided to call this off with the way he'd run off the day before. She'd been half believing there would be a call to cancel everything and send her home.

The call hadn't come though and she and her team were now at the compound, ready to resume talks.

"I hope everything turned out yesterday?" She started, hoping maybe she might get some clue as to why he'd skipped out so suddenly.

They still had no reports of any skirmishes with the ruling party or the Kazarus military. It was a big mystery and she didn't like mysteries at all during a negotiation. It left her feeling off her footing and that was the worst way to be right now.

Demir gave her a superficial smile, but she could

see strain at the edges of his eyes. Perhaps he was losing the support of his people? Maybe there was a split or faction forming she needed to be worried about?

"All is well, thank you." He gestured into the room they'd used the day before. It was a small office with tall windows that lit it well and a few armchairs where she and Demir and the advisors who were sitting in on the talks would sit. Her assistant took a seat against the wall behind her, and Heath and Duff stationed themselves outside the door.

They took up talks with discussion of the military support the US government would provide.

He was looking for more than she'd offered of course, which she'd expected.

"Training won't do us any good. Your people don't know the region, they don't know what we can accomplish. My men know this country, this land. They know how to fight. I need to see more weapons and technology from your government if we are to make this happen."

Eleanor had a feeling the men standing guard outside the door would beg to differ with his statement. They fought in this region. They knew exactly what was involved.

Still, she was focused right now on keeping peaceful talks with Demir and moving things forward. When she needed to, she would argue the point with him. For now, she had other goals.

"We can discuss the support my government might be willing to provide when we've talked about a few other topics. We need to discuss the hostages you're holding."

She very carefully didn't say she was willing to negotiate for their release. The US had made a careful distinction between negotiating with hostage takers and communicating with them. Communication was okay. Negotiation was not. Still, she wanted him to know that his action or inaction where they were concerned would affect the outcome of these talks.

He eyed her steadily, his face a blank and unreadable mask. "With the right incentive, I could be persuaded to release the US citizens."

"France and the UK are our allies," she reminded him.

"So you are here to speak for all three nations now?"

Eleanor didn't let him rattle her. She smiled. "I speak for the US but I must consider the ways that any agreement we might reach here will affect all of our relationships, and that includes the relationships with our current allies. Surely you can't expect us to throw over current allies for new ones. Were we so fickle, no one would want to align themselves with the US."

She purposefully kept the possibility of them reaching an agreement here as just that: a possibility.

She went on. "In fact, I would think you would

want to see our loyalty to those we have pledged to if you're going to enter any kind of agreement with us."

He smirked. "I'm not so naïve as to think you won't also be pledging your backing to King Barrera and his so-called-president. The United States will be hedging its bets where Kazarus is concerned."

Eleanor knew that Demir saw the president of Kazarus as nothing more than a puppet of the ruling monarchy, and he appeared to be correct in that assessment. From what their intelligence could gather, the president of Kazarus stood up and said what King Barrera wanted him to, when he wanted him to, and where he wanted him to.

Demir went on. "Your government will back both parties in Kazarus, making sure it has an ally in the event of either outcome of this war."

"My government will put its weight behind those it believes will do the most good for it in the long term. At the moment, that's looking like your party. We'd like to see a functioning successful democracy in place. We'd like that government to be strong enough to stand up to the terrorist groups preying on the people of your nation, taking advantage of the fact people are hungry and scared."

She was using some of his own words they'd found in his writings to his people and the speeches he broadcast on the internet. If she was subtle about it, without outright mimicking his words, it would go a long way toward psychologically allying him with her.

"But to support your mission, to put the enormous weight of the US government squarely in your corner, I need to see that you are truly an ally. That means not holding any of our people or our allies' people hostage for your cause. I need to see that you will be the power we hope you'll be against terrorism in the region. That you'll have the strength to stop arms being traded to Al Qaeda and ISIS or other groups that mean us harm."

She didn't mention democracy again. The US people had this idyllic view of their government. They wanted to believe the government was going around the world preaching Christianity and democracy and all that. What her government cared about here was stopping the arms trade to terrorists who presented a threat to US citizens. The fact Demir was a Christian looking to put a democracy in place in Kazarus was immaterial to that end goal.

He smiled. "Let us discuss the hostages after lunch. For now, let's talk about this military might you speak of."

She smiled and shut him down. "If we're going to talk about the hostages after lunch, I believe I'll take an early lunch. My assistant and I had no time for breakfast this morning, so this works out well. We'll go back to our hotel and return later to continue this discussion." She stood and Beth did the same.

She didn't care that they'd only been in the room thirty minutes. She wasn't playing his game. She didn't expect him to call her bluff and he didn't.

And that was fine with her. She'd return after lunch. If he wasn't ready to talk about the hostages then, she would end the talks for the day. She had time. She could take control of the talks and keep it.

She could and would. She had learned a long time ago not to let people walk all over her. She didn't care if he was the head of one of the world's largest guerrilla armies. She was only moving forward with these negotiations on her terms.

CHAPTER 15

"You hear Nan and Ris are planning to go private when they finish their tours this month?" Heath asked as he and Duff stood outside the room where the talks were taking place. They'd cleared the small room when Eleanor entered. There were no other exits and the room was an interior room of the palace-like building so it didn't have any windows.

He didn't like being posted outside, but he was coping. Barely.

Duff grunted a response.

"HALO Security. It's out of Austin. Bunch of former SEALs and Deltas," he said, not at all put off by Duff's lack of spoken reply. The man mostly communicated in grunts and hard stares.

Heath was surprised when the door opened and Eleanor and Beth walked out. They'd only been in the room for a half hour.

Heath and Duff went on alert and he saw Zip and Merlin do the same down the hall.

Eleanor gave him a small shake of her head, signaling to him that all was well, as she and Beth walked toward the exit to the building.

He and Duff fell in behind them while Zip and Merlin cleared the way ahead of them.

When they'd exited the building, Eleanor spoke to him. "We're heading back to the hotel until after lunch." She lowered her voice. "Can you have someone watch the camp and see if Demir leaves? He's not willing to discuss the hostages at all and since we know he went to the bunker yesterday I want to know if he goes over there again today."

"You don't think he'll give in and call you back to the table?" Beth asked.

Eleanor shook her head. "No. He's not going to capitulate. In fact, I'm not sure he'll give in after lunch. I need to be ready to completely walk away from here if he doesn't. He won't respect me if I don't and we'll get nowhere on this fast. We'd be better off walking away and coming back to him down the road."

They met up with the rest of Eleanor's team and were in the SUV and moving toward the exit of the compound when Beth answered. "I've never known you to walk away from a negotiation without getting what you wanted. You'd really leave if he won't deal?"

Eleanor didn't answer but Heath could see the struggle in her eyes. She wanted to get those hostages out and wanted to cut the deal her boss had sent her here to make.

She'd been like that in high school, too. Always wanting to be the best at everything she put her mind to. She'd put so much pressure on herself to succeed, her nose stuck in her books studying all the time.

He'd been the exact opposite. And he convinced her to loosen up and have fun with him for the short time they'd been together.

His gaze roved over the landscape as they drove through the sparse fir trees that dotted the landscape around Demir's compound. They were driving on what could really only be described as a sandy path, but it was wide enough for the SUV. They would hit a larger dirt road soon that would take them out to the main highway and back to the populated region where the hotel was.

As they approached the intersection with the dirt road, he couldn't miss the truck barreling toward them. He pushed Eleanor down.

"You see it, Merlin?"

"I'm not blind," the unofficial leader of their team called back to him as he swerved to the left so the truck missed them.

The rest of Eleanor's team was in the SUV behind them. The truck clipped the corner of their vehicle and they spun out.

Zip and Jangles jumped out of the vehicle as Merlin slowed. Beth was screaming and Eleanor was trying to sit up, but Heath kept himself over her. No way he was letting anything happen to her. Not when he'd just found her again.

What the hell was that thought doing there? It almost sounded like he hoped now that he'd found her, this could go somewhere. It couldn't. Yes, he'd kissed her the night before, but that didn't mean anything more could happen between them.

There wasn't room for love in his world. She would forever be waiting at home for him when he was away on missions. They couldn't tell anyone where they were going or when they'd be back. Couldn't let her know if he was safe. It would be hell on any woman who was with him. He wouldn't do that to Eleanor. Wouldn't turn her world into one of uncertainty and strain like that.

"My team?" She asked from beneath him as Merlin sped up and got their SUV out of there.

He had to hand it to her. She was handling this much better than he thought she would. Better than Beth who was still screaming.

Heath put a hand on Beth's shoulder and pushed her down, but he didn't cover her with his body. His assignment was to protect Eleanor. And assignment or not, that's what he was going to do. If they wanted to get to her, they'd have to go through him.

Merlin was driving hell bent down the dirt road now.

"My team?" Eleanor said again, this time a lot more demand in the words.

Heath looked back. Zip and Jangles had opened fire on the truck from behind a large boulder. He couldn't see if anyone had gotten out of the truck, but they were returning fire.

Duff was driving the SUV with the rest of Eleanor's team in it and he had the driver's door open, unloading his HK 416 on the truck.

"They're safe," he said to Eleanor, not really knowing for sure that they hadn't been injured in the crash. And it wasn't like they were out of danger.

Still, the crash had really been minor and he fully expected Duff and the boys to take care of the people in the truck and get her team back to the hotel in one piece. It's what they did and they were good at it.

"We're not going back for them?" There was outrage in her voice.

Beth was crying now.

"No," Heath said, no apology at all in the words. "Our mission is to keep you safe. Our team has them covered."

He looked behind them. There were no signs of anyone else coming at them or anyone coming to help the guys in the truck. He watched as Zip and Jangles approached the cab of the truck.

Seconds later, they were hopping into the SUV with the others and Duff was steering the dented vehicle around the truck to catch up to Heath and Merlin.

"They're safe," he said to her and Beth. "Catching up now."

He eased back and let Eleanor sit up.

She turned to look out the back window. The SUV was still a long ways back but it was clear they were catching up and the truck wasn't pursuing them.

He could hear her exhalation as she let out a relieved breath. He squeezed her thigh as he started to realize just how much his heart was slamming in his chest. He was trained to handle combat situations and life-threatening scenarios. He was used to holding the life of someone they were tasked to protect in his hands. Used to split second decisions and to the adrenaline pumping scenarios where you went from copasetic to FUBAR in an instant.

He stayed calm and steady through it all. He didn't worry. He did the job.

But he'd never felt the way he did on this mission. Every time Eleanor was in danger it sent him reeling. He'd never felt the heart stopping terror he felt now at the thought of her being hurt or worse.

He didn't like that whoever was trying to stop this negotiation had tried for her again.

"Is my team okay?" Eleanor asked.

Merlin nodded, giving her the update that had come over their earpiece moments before. "No one is seriously injured. Marcus hit his head and Sharon's wrist is sore but nothing life threatening."

"How did they know we were coming?" Eleanor

looked at Heath. "We were scheduled to be there through the afternoon."

Merlin met Heath's gaze in the rearview mirror. Heath had been wondering the same thing.

Still, he brushed off her concern. She had enough to think about without worrying about the fact that someone on her team might be trying to get her killed.

"They probably had a team watching for any opportunity that might arise."

It was true. They'd probably simply left the men there to watch just in case they got a shot in on her. In fact, the attempt hadn't been all that professional or well organized. Heath wondered if the organization after her had simply hired a few extra amateurs to cover their bases since the professional teams they'd sent so far hadn't been successful.

What he didn't say to her was that it was possible the person who had leaked her flight information wasn't back in her home office, but here on the ground with them. And that person had somehow messaged their contact when Eleanor changed their schedule.

When he got her back to the hotel safely, Heath was going to tear into the lives of the people around her. They needed to find out who was helping these people and put a stop to it. Now.

CHAPTER 16

Not unexpectedly, it was a while before he was able to get Eleanor alone. She met with her team while his people tried to find out what was happening. Duff radioed in that Demir and his brother had gone to the bunker where the doctors were being kept. Duff was still watching from outside, but so far no one had come back out.

He studied the people sitting at the table with her now. Marcus's hands were shaking and the others all looked shook up. But even if one of them had been the one to tip off whoever was gunning for them, they'd be shaken by what had happened.

He could see Beth looking at all of the members of the team and could all but read her thoughts. She was starting to doubt all of them. Geoff too, going by the edge to his tone as they spoke.

Eleanor, though, she was holding it all together.

"Guys, we have a job to do. I know what just happened was scary as hell and if any of you want to go home, I won't blame you for that. But if we stay, we need to find a way to stay calm through this and go back in there. We can't let whoever this is derail these talks. We just can't."

Sharon rubbed her arms as though she were trying to warm herself. "That was ... " She stopped and shook her head. "That was horrible. It was terrifying when that truck hit us."

Eleanor reached over and squeezed the other woman's hand. "It was. And I know this is hard. You can go home if that's what you want to do." She looked to her people. "And you guys can stay back at the hotel and support me from here if you want to do that, too. I can manage."

That got her people's attention and Heath saw steel in all their eyes at that. Even Marcus, despite the shaky hands.

"To hell with that," Beth said. "We're not going to be run off." She looked around at the group. "And I'll tell you what I'm also not going to let them do. I won't let someone make me suspect all of you. I don't believe it was anyone in this room and I won't let someone scare me into thinking the worst of the people I know and trust to have my back."

Eleanor was smiling at Beth but Heath wasn't so sure. He wouldn't rule out anyone as long as Eleanor was in danger. He couldn't.

Half an hour later, Heath watched as Jangles and Zip led Eleanor's people out of the hotel room before turning to Eleanor.

"Want to go to our room and take a break? You can lie down for a bit before meeting the others for dinner."

She tilted her head. "So it's officially *our* room?"

He gave a low laugh and walked closer to her, closing the space between them like he'd wanted to all day. He'd never had such a hard time remaining professional on an op. Not that he was fully succeeding. He'd already made it damned good and clear to his team that they were all welcome to take turns standing watch at Eleanor's door, but that he'd be the only one in that room overnight with her.

He opened the door to the attached room and they did the same routine they'd done the night before when they'd gone down the hall. They returned to the room they'd slept in, this time with Jangles opening the door and leaving when they entered.

Heath watched as she kicked off her shoes and went to the bed. When he went to the armchair and started to lower himself into it, she stopped him.

"Are you planning to rest?"

He nodded. He normally wouldn't be kicking off his boots and laying down to rest, even if that's what this time was for. He and his men were still on guard. But he knew Jangles was outside the room and Duff and Merlin were in the room next door and he'd been up much of the night before. They were covered and he needed to rest if he was going to be any use to Eleanor.

He groaned at the idea of being of use to her. Damn, he wanted to let her use him any and every way she wanted to. He pictured her above him, straddling him as she sank down onto him. Running her hands over his chest as her breasts swayed above him.

Christ.

"Then share the bed with me. That chair can't be comfortable."

He kept his face blank even though his eyebrows wanted to climb onto his forehead at her words. "The bed?"

Okay, so he hadn't quite managed to keep his voice from going thick and heavy at the suggestion of sharing the bed with her.

"We're adults, Heath. I think we can manage to lay on a bed for a nap together."

He wasn't so sure about that, but he didn't argue. He shucked his boots and laid on the bed, over the covers like she was doing.

He wanted to take Nori into his arms the way he used to and felt his chest tighten at the memory of her arms wrapped around him and the way she used to snuggle into him, burying her head in his chest.

She and her team had just pulled apart the entire morning's negotiations so he searched for a topic that wasn't at all related to work.

"Tell me about your stepfather. You said you took his name when you were in college?"

Heath knew her mom had worked two jobs to support her and Eleanor growing up. Her mom had been young when she had her and her father had never been part of the picture, but her mom had worked hard to make sure Eleanor had everything she needed, including her mom's love.

He remembered going over to their small apartment. Eleanor had her own room but her mom slept on a small bed in what was supposed to be a tiny office in the one-bedroom apartment. Even as a teenager, he'd been able to see that her mom was something special. She wanted the best for Eleanor and she didn't want Eleanor to have to work. She always told Eleanor she should be able to focus on school, not making sure they had food. He had respected the hell out of Eleanor's mom.

Eleanor nodded against his chest. "My mom married him when I was a freshman in college. He didn't care if I was already grown up. He was there with my mom for all the important things. Dropping me at school, parent weekends, that kind of thing. And when I came home for breaks, he wanted to hang out. Not in an I'm-trying-too-hard kind of way. He just was there for me as though he'd been with my mom and me forever. And for once, I saw that my mom wasn't having to work as hard anymore. She had a partner in things. It was nice."

"It sounds nice," he said. He had never gotten along with his own dad so what she was describing with her stepdad really did hit home. Heath would have loved to have a parent that took an interest in him like that.

She nodded. "And then when my mom got sick, he was by her side all the time. He never left her, never seemed to mind taking care of her. He was her cheerleader all the way."

"That's good that she had someone with her through it all." He wanted to reach over and hold her, but he stuck his hands behind his head and clenched them together, like lacing the fingers might lock them in place to keep him from doing something stupid. "And you. It's nice that you had him there with you when she was sick."

"It was. I wanted to leave school to help her but they wouldn't hear of it. At first I was resentful of that. It had always been the two of us and when he came along, I was okay with that because I didn't want her to be lonely. But then when she was sick, I kind of wanted to be the one to be by her side."

"Did you leave school to be with her?"

"No." She had rolled to face him and the move was damned distracting, but he wanted to hear this. Wanted to know all of what he'd missed when they had been living separate lives.

She went on. "He convinced me not to. He told me he would always be there for her and for me. He wanted me to do what my mom would want, and that was to stay in school. He promised me that if she started to lose her fight with cancer, he would let me know so I could come home and be there at the end."

"And he did?"

She nodded again, into his chest. "I came home for the last few weeks. It was then that he told me he wanted me to take his name, if I wanted to. That even though I was almost ready to graduate college by then, that he and I were family and we would stay that way even after my mom died."

"Are you still close?"

"Yes. Very. By that time, I really did love him like a dad and I cried when he asked me if I would take his name. It meant so much to me and I know it meant the world to my mom to know I wouldn't be alone after she died. He's remarried now and has step-kids and grand-step-kids and all. I still go see them sometimes when I can get away and I spend holidays there when I'm in the states."

"Where do they live?"

"Texas. Austin. It's a fun place to visit." She was tilting her head up to him now and he would swear she was staring at his mouth.

He knew he was going to give in and kiss her any minute. Knew he was past winning this fight. He was too far gone. But he wanted her to know one thing.

"You were incredible at the compound with Demir today. He saw you as a real equal. I could see that he developed respect for you as the morning went on and you showed him how in command you were. How you could go into this compound in a country in the middle of a civil war and keep your cool and negotiate with him. You did good, Nori. Real good."

She flushed and ducked her head and he laughed.

Then he leaned closer, closing the distance between them, careful to keep some small amount of space between their bodies even as his mouth found hers. If he didn't, he wouldn't be able to stop this with a kiss. Wouldn't be able to leave it at that. But he had to taste her. Had to show her what she did to him.

He kissed her long and slow and deep. He just wanted the chance to connect with her. To be with her in this way, with just the two of them. To let her feel how much he'd missed her in his life all these years. How much her absence had cut him, even when he hadn't known that was what was missing.

CHAPTER 17

Zip and Jangles were watching Eleanor. It was the only way Heath would agree to leave her. He trusted his team with his life and hers even though it killed him not to be with her. But for now, he needed to be here with Merlin and Duff, poring over the particulars of the reports they'd gotten on Eleanor's team members.

"I don't see anything that jumps out," Merlin said and Duff nodded his agreement.

Heath had to agree with them. He was really hoping they'd find something obvious. A gambling problem or large deposit of money.

"Sharon Geiger is the newest person in their office, but she's been with the foreign service for ten years. Exemplary record." Merlin shuffled the pages in front of him.

"I don't like Geoff." Heath stood and paced as he spoke. "The guy is always asking for details on where

131

we'll be going and how things are going to work when we're getting ready to move."

Duff shook his head. "According to Eleanor, he didn't have access to her flight information. Only Marcus and Beth had that information."

Heath shook his head. "Marcus or Beth could have easily shared that information. They'd have had no reason to hold that back from another member of their team."

Merlin looked at him. "You sure you're being objective here? I've seen you glaring at Geoff when he asks Eleanor if she wants to join them for dinner."

Heath probably shouldn't have let the small growl slip from his lips, but Merlin was right. The guy really was bothering Heath. Eleanor might not see it but Geoff was hitting on her.

"He shouldn't be making a pass at her. She's his boss."

Duff laughed, earning a glare from Heath.

It was Merlin who answered, though. "I'm pretty sure that pass you're talking about is called politeness and manners, big guy. You're seeing shit that isn't here where Eleanor Bonham is concerned."

Heath turned on the two men, his chest filling with anger at the accusation. They didn't understand. Couldn't understand.

Eleanor wasn't just a job to him. She meant something and even if he couldn't let that go anywhere past these next few days, he damned sure wasn't going to let anything happen to her.

If that meant he saw danger everywhere he looked for now, so be it.

Merlin raised his hands in surrender but Heath saw amusement in his expression.

His anger dissipated. They were just razzing him. They had his back.

Duff had been tapping away on his computer but he looked up now. "Sharon has a sick mom. She requires a lot of care and I don't see where the money is coming from for that. She's in a high-end assisted living home in DC. It's possible someone is paying for that care in exchange for Sharon's help?"

Heath turned to the door, but Merlin was standing in his way.

He crossed his arms and looked at the unofficial head of their team. "We need to question her."

Merlin put a hand up. "Take a step back from this. Let me question her while you go sit with Eleanor. You're of no use to us like this. Let us handle looking into who might be after her and who might be feeding them information."

Heath went hands on hips and shook his head. "I want to be in on the questioning. When we go back to the talks, we can't go back with this leak in tow."

He saw Merlin and Duff exchange a look but Merlin acquiesced, giving a small nod.

Merlin stood. "Duff, you stay on the research while Woof and I pull Sharon out of there and talk to her."

Heath ignored the look Eleanor gave him when they asked Sharon to leave the brainstorming session with the team minutes later. They led Sharon down the hall to one of their empty rooms. If he had anything to do with it, when Eleanor and the team went back to the camp later that afternoon, she wouldn't be taking the traitor with her.

"What is it?" the dark-haired woman asked, her blue eyes going wide. "Has something else happened?"

Merlin pulled out a chair and gestured to it in the small hotel room. The tight space worked well for the situation. They wanted Sharon feeling the pressure and putting her in tight quarters with two who were trained to kill with nothing more than their hands was one way to do that.

If she wasn't their leak, he'd apologize, but until he knew for sure, he wasn't going to pull punches and coddle Eleanor's team.

"Tell us about your mom, Sharon," Heath said. It wasn't a gentle suggesting. He put menace behind the words.

Uneasy didn't begin to describe the look that crossed her face as she glanced at the door of the room.

"My mom?" Sharon looked from Heath to Merlin and back. Then she stood suddenly. "Is my mom okay? What happened?"

She wasn't looking like someone who was guilty of

134

working with the enemy, but he wasn't ready to take her off their list yet. People can be damn good liars and anyone who would be feeding information about Eleanor's whereabouts to the people trying to take her out had to be damn good at lying to have gotten this far.

Merlin went with the good cop here, probably knowing Heath didn't have it in him just then.

"Your mom is fine, Sharon. Have a seat." Merlin put the sympathetic hand on Sharon's shoulder. "Nothing's happened to your mom. We just need to know a little about her care."

Sharon's brow furrowed and she shook her head. "I don't understand. Why do you need to know about my mom's care?"

Heath answered. "She's in a very expensive care home, isn't she? Do you want to tell us who's paying that bill for you?"

He watched as understanding dawned on her face.

It was followed quickly by anger. "You think I'm the one selling information about Eleanor. You think I'm working with whoever's been trying to hurt her." Her eyes flashed and she looked ready to take their heads off. "I would never hurt Eleanor that way. Never."

Merlin pulled the chair over and sat opposite Sharon. His voice was soft when he spoke. "We have to go through everybody Sharon, tear apart everybody's lives. It's something that has to be done. Even if it's just to rule you out so we can find the person who is doing this to her, we need to make this happen so we can move on and find the right person. You understand that, don't you?"

Sharon nodded, just as Merlin had wanted her to. Heath knew Merlin wanted her agreeing with him so that when it came time, she agreed to answer his questions, too.

Merlin continued. "You know how important it is that we stop these people, right?"

She nodded again.

"And you know how important it is that these talks aren't derailed, don't you?"

Another nod.

"Help us out. Let us cross you off the list. That's all we want," Merlin said. "Tell us how your mom's care is being paid. When Duff was looking through your files, the cost of your mom's care home stands out as a pretty major expense. You understand we have to account for that."

Sharon sighed. "My brother pays for her care and I don't ask how he does it." She looked away, wrapping her arms around her middle.

"I should ask, but I don't because my mom needs the home and the medicine and physical therapy she gets there. My brother has never been one to follow the rules, and more and more I'm pretty sure he's not really living off honest money right now. But I don't have any contact with him, I've got nothing to do with whatever he's doing. He pays the bills and that's all I know. So it's

She was beginning to wonder if there was more to his taking doctors and nurses than the simple fact that they had been in country and available to be grabbed. She needed to talk to her people back in the office. There had to be more going on here than any of the analysts had discovered yet and she needed them hunting down that information if she was going to have a shot at being successful here.

"Set up the video call and I'll see what I can do. I can't make any promises, though. I can almost guarantee you my boss is going to want me to have eyes on those doctors and nurses in person before this goes any further."

Demir waved a hand to one of his people and spoke quietly to him when he came over.

Then he looked up at Eleanor. "Why don't we break while the video call is being set up?"

Eleanor held in a sigh. At this rate they were doing more breaking than talking during these negotiations. It was part of the reason her gut was telling her something was off with this whole thing. If they didn't have more than one reason for wanting to support the overthrow of the current regime in Kazarus, she might tell her boss this wasn't going to go anywhere.

But these talks could very well be the key to stopping a resurgence of ISIS and Al Qaeda. And she'd be damned if she would shut down anything that gave them a chance of doing that before she tried everything in her power to make it happen.

She would keep at this as long as she could to see if she could make headway with Demir. Headway that would keep dangerous weapons out of the hands of ISIS and Al Qaeda.

CHAPTER 19

"I don't like it," Marcus said.

"Then we're in agreement," Eleanor said as she turned to Heath and his team. "Did any of you see anything on the video feed that makes you think our intel is wrong about where the doctors and nurses are being held?"

They all shook their heads. There hadn't been much to see in the background when they talked to the hostages. Nothing more than a basic room that might or might not be part of the bunker. Its walls had looked like plaster but they could be plaster over concrete in a bunker or they could be the plaster walls of any windowless room in any country. Hell, for that matter, they could be on this compound in a building right next door.

The hostages hadn't been able to talk much and the video feed hadn't been long, but from what she could see they were in good health. They didn't look like they'd been starved or tortured or anything along those lines. But she had felt like they were trying to convey something to her with their eyes. She just didn't know what.

"His request for access to US military satellites is completely off-the-wall," said Geoff.

"I agree. I can't for the life of me figure out why he thinks that's something we could offer," Eleanor said.

"Maybe he doesn't," Heath said.

Eleanor turned to him. "What you mean?"

"Maybe he knows it's an impossible ask but he also knows that you'll need to take it to your boss before you can officially turn him down. He had to know you wouldn't have come here with prior authorization to put satellite intelligence on the table. So it would take you some time to run it up the pipeline."

"And time is what he wants." Eleanor closed his eyes. "He's playing us. He wants to delay for something and I guarantee you it's something that has to do with those hostages."

"But what? And why did he agree to these talks if he's just going to screw around like this?" Marcus asked.

Eleanor shook her head. She didn't know. And she hated feeling so out of her depth in an arena where she should have been in complete control.

CHAPTER 20

Eleanor and Demir spent the following morning working out the details of the weapons and training support the US would provide to Demir's army. They also negotiated for medical support and food for his people.

The stronger his people were, the more likely his efforts in the area were to succeed, so medical care and food were an important part of his plans.

She had met his mother and father earlier in the day, confirming for her that this man's family was important to him. His father walked with a severe limp and she learned it was the result of the battle that killed Demir's grandfather when King Barrera's regime overthrew his predecessor's party.

As far as Demir and his family were concerned, they were attempting to right old wrongs with their fight against King Barrera. Their's was a battle to return the country to the rightful hands of the people.

Their conversation so far had convinced Eleanor that Demir wouldn't slaughter or persecute the Muslim population of Kazarus if his army succeeded in toppling the current regime. She only prayed she was right about that and was reading him correctly.

But as things stood now, Christians in Kazarus were being oppressed and in many cases worse so she had to hope that her efforts here would help put an end to that without flipping the situation from one religious sect to another.

"I think we are close to an agreement, wouldn't you say, Ms. Bonham?" Demir asked.

"We're close. And I'm truly hoping we'll be able to commit to an agreement here today," Eleanor said. She meant it.

Demir smiled. "There is the matter of the satellite access."

Eleanor tilted her head. "And the hostages."

Demir gave a slight shrug as if to say they were unimportant and Eleanor had to wonder if she was putting more faith in this man than she should. "Yes, the hostages," he seemed to add almost grudgingly.

"I can't offer you on-demand satellite access anytime you want. I'm sure you understand our country can't simply put our military satellites at your disposal. What I can offer you is a one time still image of Kazarus, everything we have access to from our satellites at this moment in time. You'll know where the government has military forces, and the level of forces you're going up against, where the king might be holding his largest weapons. It'll give you an enormous advantage you don't currently have."

Demir was shaking his head. "You know as well as I do that forces change locations routinely. The regime can move troops from one area to another in a matter of days. A one-shot moment in time tells me nothing."

"It tells you a great deal more than you know at the moment."

He looked at her, waiting, and Eleanor weighed how much she could give to him.

"If the hostages are released safely in the following 24 hours, I'll see that you get satellite images taken immediately after that and an additional set of satellite images at a time of your choosing. This is a one-time offer that won't be made again."

She could see his hesitation and had to wonder again why it was so important that he hold onto these hostages.

"I'm going to need to speak with my brother before I can agree to this."

Eleanor had to admit the statement shocked her. She knew Farid was his right-hand man, but she honestly hadn't thought Demir would defer to him in any way and the way he just said that made it sound as though his brother was going to be offering more than

147

simply counsel on the decision. She kept her face blank as she nodded.

It was possible Demir was using his brother as a delaying tactic. Why had he opened these talks if he was only going to delay her at every turn?

"I can give you until this evening and then the offer is rescinded and our talks will be closed." She paused making sure she had his full attention. "If I leave this country without an agreement, we won't reopen negotiations. This is a one-shot deal for you and your people."

As Eleanor left the room she wondered if she should've already closed these talks and walked away. This had been off from the start and it didn't seem to be getting any better as time went on.

CHAPTER 21

Eleanor felt the frustration of the day build to a boiling point. Luckily for her, Heath had finally put an end to it, whisking her out of the room where she'd been rehashing the day's events with her team.

She felt the relief wash over her when she and Heath entered what she now thought of as their room.

She kicked off her shoes and turned to face him, but instead of finding him across the room at the door, she found he was standing inches away from her. Eleanor's whole body tightened with awareness. When this man was near her, everything in her called out to close the distance between them, to come together like they used to years before.

She wanted that again. Maybe it was the tension of the situation. Maybe it was just their past. Or maybe it was the fact she'd never met a man who did more to turn her on without even trying than this man.

He met her eyes and she saw the heat in them. Heat and desire she felt powerless to fight against. Who was she kidding? She didn't want to fight against this.

His eyes ran over her body, heating her with nothing more than his look. "You're so fucking sexy, Nori. It's been all I can do to keep my hands off you from the minute I saw you again."

She blinked up at him. Was he really saying these things to her? She licked her lips and saw his eyes flare, focused on her mouth.

His voice was husky with desire. "You okay with us taking advantage of the fact we'll be together for another night before this is all over and we have to go back to our lives?"

She wouldn't say no to that. Couldn't say no to that.

She'd had a few boyfriends after him in college and she sometimes dated here and there, but truth be told, she worked too damned much. She didn't take the time for a relationship or, frankly, even a one-night-stand.

And she hadn't realized until now how much she missed that. So, yes, she was definitely okay with this.

"I want you so damned much I can taste you on my tongue, feel you in my hands. I fucking need to touch you, Nori, but I need you to know it can't go anywhere," he said. "I'm just not that guy. But we have these few days."

If even that. They would likely be leaving her in the next day or two. "It works for me if it works for you," she said. "For whatever time we're together for this mission and then we go back to our own lives." She wasn't surprised to find her voice was as husky as his had been.

And he hadn't even touched her yet.

She was shaking when he reached his hands out to touch her, his hands barely fluttering over her skin as he skimmed her neck, then cradled her face. Her whole body went soft for him. She could feel herself getting wet with desire at the barest of touches from him.

He leaned in and kissed the column of her neck, speaking softly against her skin. "It damned near killed me waiting for that meeting to be over so I could get you alone."

She tilted her head back to meet his eyes. "Yeah?" She challenged. "Show me."

Permission granted, he pulled the sling off his arm, wincing only slightly at the movement. She opened her mouth to object that maybe they shouldn't do this with his arm still injured, but he was moving her back toward the bed.

She sank onto it and lay back, spreading her legs to make room for him as he came down over her. Some part of her wanted this to be slow and easy but there was a bigger part of her that wanted his clothes off yesterday and him inside her two days before that.

She wrapped her legs around his thighs and ground up into him, drawing a growl in response. Her hands found the waist band of his pants and tugged his shirt so she could get under his clothes to the smooth expanse of skin she knew she'd find there.

He broke their kiss as he reached and tugged his shirt up and over his head. And Lord, she was in heaven.

She ran her hands over taut muscles and tanned skin before trailing her fingers through the light smattering of hair on his chest.

"I love the way your hands feel on me, Nori. Love you touching me like this. Nothing has ever felt like your touch. Not in all these years."

She wanted to whimper at his words. She wanted more with him. She knew she shouldn't but her heart wanted it with an ache that was real and harsh and so damned hard to shove aside.

But she did. Because if she could just put aside her foolish dreams for more with him, she'd at least have this with him. She would at least have this moment. She would have this to remember when she went home and she lost him again.

He was pulling her shirt up and she broke away long enough to let him get it over her head.

Then his mouth was on her breast and the heat of his touch through the lace of her bra was erotic and tantalizing. He moved to the other breast, this time, lifting it from the cup so he could get to her skin.

Eleanor laughed which made Heath growl at her.

"Sorry," she panted. "It's just that you would think

we'd learned how to slow down now that we're not teenagers."

"There's no going slow where you're concerned, Nori. Never has been."

Heath stood and had his pants and boxers off in seconds before tugging at her pants. She did little to help him. She couldn't. She was struck dumb at the sight of him before her, completely nude.

He had always been well muscled and all that as a teenager. But damn, he'd been nothing like this. This man before her had muscles in places she didn't know a man could and his body bore the evidence of long hard days doing things most men couldn't do.

Tanned legs and muscular thighs went to a torso that could have been sculpted of stone. His shoulders were broad and looked like they could hold the weight of a thousand worlds with little effort. He was perfection.

And there, hers for the taking, was an erection that proved that even though she'd aged and wasn't exactly a gym rat, he was equally as aroused by her as she was by him.

She reached for his erection, wrapping her hand tightly around the silken hardness. He was perfection.

He caught her mouth in a kiss again and his hands found her, slipping into the waistband of her panties, going straight to where she needed him most.

She felt him grin against her mouth. "So damned

wet, Nori. You have no idea what that does to me to know you're so ready for me."

He reached for his pants and pulled a condom from one of the pockets. As Eleanor watched him put it on, she didn't allow herself to wonder how often he did this. She didn't want to think about him with other women.

She didn't have room in her life for relationships and she had no real claim on him, but still she felt like she wanted to growl like he was always doing when she pictured him with any other woman.

She took her own clothes off as quickly as she could and then lay back on the bed and watched him, her mouth watering as he came down on top of her and his shaft found her center. He held himself there, hovering at the entrance to tease and taunt in a way that was maddening. When he dipped his head to kiss her but still didn't enter her, she wriggled and thrust her hips up trying to get him to give her what she so desperately needed.

God, she needed him with a desperation she never thought she'd feel with a man.

He groaned and slid himself into her, an inch, two. So damned slowly, she whimpered.

"Please, Heath," she said on a gasping breath. "More."

"More?" He teased even as he pushed into her another two inches before pulling back out.

"Heath." This time it was more command than plea

and he listened, driving into her with one smooth motion that sent her muscles tightening around him.

She wrapped her arms and legs around him, pulling him close as he kissed her. She thrust her hips with every thrust of his own, wanting him deeper, harder, more.

She wanted everything from this man.

He bit her lower lip as one hand went to her nipple to pinch and she was done. She climaxed hard and seconds later, she felt him thicken and come inside her but he didn't stop pumping into her as she cried out.

He captured her cry with his mouth and slowed his strokes as her muscles continued to tense in orgasm.

He collapsed on top of her in a heap. A heap she reveled in, the weight of him pressing down on her as she kept herself wrapped around him. She didn't want this to end. Didn't want to go to sleep because that would mean waking up to the reality of her doing a job that would put an end to this escape they'd found together.

If she did her job well, this would end in a matter of days. And with the end of the trip, she would lose him. Again.

CHAPTER 22

Heath had been awake more than an hour just holding Eleanor. She stirred in his arms. Since it was only three in the morning, he knew he should let her sleep. He moved to pull back, to let her roll over and fall back to sleep, but she had other ideas, apparently.

She ran a hand up his chest and began to kiss the tattoo over his right pec. It wasn't anything that would identify him as military or special forces. That could lead to torture if he was ever captured or blow his cover when he went in someplace with a false identity.

This was Kermit the frog. Kermit made him smile so it was what he'd put on his chest. Ms. Piggy was on his shoulder blade.

Of course, at the moment with the way she was running her tongue over Kermit, it was doing a hell of a lot more than make him smile. His whole body hardened, going on alert and screaming for him to roll her under him and take her again and again until she screamed his name.

"Damn, woman. You need to sleep."

"Do you want me to go to sleep?" she asked, all innocence and sunshine in her tone.

"God, no."

She laughed at that and he ran his hands over her body. He'd always loved her body. She said she was too skinny and he guessed some guys might think that. But he wouldn't change a thing about her. She was long and lithe, but still soft just where she should be. Soft enough for him to lose himself in the feel of her.

And at the moment, she was melting into his touch and he was powerless to get up and walk away. To give her the rest he knew she needed.

"Nori," he rasped out.

This time, he planned to love her slowly, thoroughly, wringing every ounce of pleasure from her before taking his own.

He rolled on top of her, keeping his weight on his good arm as he worked his mouth down her body. He trailed his tongue over her collar bone before finding his way to one breast. It shouldn't be so damned enticing when he ran his tongue over the peaked nipple, but it was.

He let his teeth catch her soft skin gently and was rewarded with her moans and pants as he made his way south.

"Heath," she whispered wriggling beneath his touch.

He slid a finger into her and covered her clitoris with his mouth. He was rock hard but he didn't want satisfaction in that moment. He wanted to hear her come. Wanted to feel her body wracked with an orgasm as he worked her with his tongue. Wanted to know he was doing that to her, that she was coming just for him.

Her hands gripped his shoulders and he added another finger, smiling when she rocked up into his hand, seeking release.

He sucked hard on her clit and she came apart, writhing and crying his name.

His reaction was so much more than physical. Yes he was ready for her, wanting to take her more than he'd ever wanted anything with another woman. But there was so much more than that. He felt the pleasure at making her orgasm deep in his chest. There was male pride, but there was also a tenderness he hadn't expected, a desire to always give her all she craved and more.

She pulled at him and he came up, reaching for one of the condoms he'd placed by the bed earlier. And then he was easing into her, sinking home to heaven.

She cradled his face in her hands and he leaned in and kissed her. He was lost to her as he began to move within her. Lost to this woman who had somehow captured his heart and hadn't let go.

Neither of them spoke as he made love to her. Neither of them said any more. They didn't need to. He saw in her eyes all she wanted to say and he opened himself to her, for once not trying to mask what he was thinking and feeling.

They had no future but that didn't change that what he felt right now was something damned close to love for this woman.

No screw that. It was love for her. He knew that. He just couldn't act on it.

And as they climaxed together he stupidly thought that maybe, just maybe, he was seeing the same thing in her eyes. That maybe she felt more for him than she was willing to admit. And didn't his stupid heart do a little belly flop right there in his chest at the thought.

CHAPTER 23

It bothered Heath a hell of a lot that they didn't know who was leaking information yet. He'd been watching Merlin question Geoff for the last half hour. They were getting nowhere.

Sharon's story had checked out. Her brother was into some shit that could definitely get him the kind of cash his mother needed. But since he was just selling drugs back in the US, it wasn't something their team would be involved with taking care of. And from what they found out, DC vice was already on to him and close to making an arrest of him and several other of the people around him.

Merlin sent Geoff back to the group with Duff following along behind him to grab Marcus next. So far Marcus, Geoff, and Beth all looked squeaky clean as far as cash inflow went. And from what they could find out, none of them had any serious vices like gambling or drug use that might lead to someone being able to pressure them into spilling secrets.

It was entirely possible whoever had leaked information was back in the office away from all of what was happening. So far they knew someone had leaked the information about Eleanor's flight and that was how she was found at the airport. But everything else could be explained without the involvement of someone on the team. They had planted a tracker on her at the airport, which was how they found Heath and her at the safe house. The next attack had taken place when they were leaving Demir's compound and it was entirely possible that truck had simply been lying in wait, watching for them to leave.

Marcus entered with Duff, looking sufficiently nervous. Duff had that effect on people. He was built like a tank and didn't talk much. It was funny how his silence made people want to blurt out all their secrets.

"I don't know what I can tell you guys," Marcus offered before they even showed him to a seat.

He looked around at them, his gaze darting from one to the next without holding on any of them.

"Have a seat, Marcus," Merlin said. "We just want to talk."

Heath didn't want to talk. He wanted to tear through everyone involved until he could figure out who had put Eleanor in danger like this.

Luckily for Marcus, Heath wasn't in charge of this interrogation.

Merlin sat across from Marcus, leaning one arm on the table next to him like they were just going to have a little chat. Merlin could go from good guy to bad guy in a heartbeat and had the ability to play out either role depending on what they were looking for with the suspect.

"We're just talking to everybody in case you've seen or heard something you don't realize might help. Sometimes that happens, you know? You overhear something but don't realize that something is anything when it's taken out of context."

"Oh, okay." Marcus was nodding now, just like Merlin wanted him to. A nodding and agreeable interviewee was one you could get information out of.

"So how about it, Marcus? Have you heard anything you thought was unusual in the last week? Or maybe somebody on your team or somebody back in the home office has been acting off? Maybe asking questions they shouldn't be or hinting around about where you guys were going or what your assignment was?"

The nodding switched to headshaking. "I haven't seen or heard anything. Nothing like that," Marcus said. "Everybody on the team has been freaked out by what's been happening. Yeah, we're in the foreign service and all, but our jobs don't usually put us in this much danger. We're usually behind a desk."

"Maybe you didn't want to come on this assignment?" Merlin asked. "Maybe you let somebody know when Eleanor was going to get off that plane hoping that she might just be scared by what happened. Scared enough to go home instead of going through with the negotiations. Since you weren't coming into the country until later, that little bit of information wouldn't put you in any danger, but it would make sure you wouldn't have to keep going with the assignment if she got scared off."

Marcus looked like he might be sick, but he was shaking his head. "I wouldn't do that." Now he looked to Heath. "I like Eleanor. I mean not like that. Not like you do. But I mean I like her. I respect her. I would never put her in danger."

He wanted to growl at even the mention of another man liking Eleanor despite the fact that Marcus was doing his best to deny that his feelings were anything similar to Heath's feelings for her.

And it sucked that he was so damn transparent that clearly Eleanor's team could see through him with no trouble at all.

Fantastic. He hoped like hell they didn't look down on her or see her as anything less than professional because of him.

Duff stepped closer to Marcus. "Sometimes you can like a person, but still be willing to take a little extra cash if you were assured that person wouldn't really be hurt. Maybe somebody told you they were just trying to scare Eleanor and you thought, what could it hurt to make a little money on the side if she's not going to get hurt?"

Marcus turned an even darker shade of green. He continued shaking his head and seemed to be looking at Heath for help.

Heath blew out a long breath. He was more and more convinced that whoever had leaked the information about Eleanor's flight wasn't on this team. Wasn't in country with them.

Eleanor had assured them that she was close to making an agreement happen with Demir. She was pretty sure they would have the release of the hostages within the next 24 hours, and she and Demir would be signing off on terms that would get the US one step closer to ridding the region of ISIS and Al Qaeda. Or at least hamstringing the organizations enough that they weren't able to do the kind of damage they had in past years.

They all wanted to see that happen. They all wanted to see the terrorist bastards who had done so much harm and spread so much of their sick twisted message go down.

The secure sat phone lit up and he and his teammates shared a look that said they agreed this questioning was going nowhere.

"Okay Marcus," Merlin said, standing, "we'll let you head on back to the rest of the group. We'll be going back to the compound soon."

Duff walked Marcus back to the room where Eleanor and her team were waiting with Jangles and Zip watching them.

Merlin picked up the sat phone and answered while Heath tried to calm the frustration coursing through him. He hated thinking that the closer they got to an agreement with Demir the more likely it was that the attacks on Eleanor would increase.

"Yes, sir. Understood." Merlin switched off the phone and set it down, turning to look at Heath.

"What is it?" Heath had a sinking feeling in his gut.

"State Department is putting a backup plan in place. They aren't convinced the talks are going to get them where they need to be on this and there's pressure from a lot of people to get those doctors and nurses out of there."

"And?" Heath asked, knowing there was more. Eleanor would be pissed if they pulled the plug on her talks.

Merlin continued. "They've pulled in Delta Team Two. They'd been doing recon on the bunker for the last twelve hours. They're ready to move with us backing them if the talks don't pan out."

He was talking about a team they were good friends with and had done a lot of work with in the past, Delta Team Two. Trigger, Lefty, Brain, Oz, Lucky, Doc, and Grover were damned good men.

Men Heath would want beside him on any mission. Still, he knew this conversation wasn't headed in a direction he was going to like.

Heath wanted to rail about them not knowing this was happening all this time, but the military was like that. If they wanted shit compartmentalized they did it and no one got to tell them to fuck off for it. You didn't get to tell Uncle Sam to fuck off.

He thought of all Eleanor had put into these talks. She'd put her life on the line for them. And it was all about to fall to shit.

CHAPTER 24

Eleanor was on the phone with her boss when Heath entered the room. Her team was watching her from the table and she could tell they'd picked up on the fact something was wrong.

Which was putting it mildly.

"You can't talk them out of this?" She asked Cheryl, knowing Cheryl would have already done all she could.

"Deputy Director Hughes is pushing hard. He's got enough support from the Joint Chiefs at this point to back the raid."

"When is it going to happen?"

"All I know is that it will be in the next twenty-four hours. It's up to the Delta team on the ground to decide when they move in."

Eleanor turned away from Heath. "Then I need to go back in there. If I don't, Demir will know something's up and he'll put more people on the hostages."

She could hear Cheryl's sigh on the other end so she pressed her point.

"Besides, if I can get an agreement in place, we don't need to put anyone at risk going in. I'm close, Cheryl. It's not too late to salvage this."

Eleanor heard Heath's curse behind her. She didn't dare look at him. She would battle this out with her boss.

"You know I'm right Cheryl. It's the right thing to do. We need this agreement to stop the chain of weapons heading into terrorist hands. If we can make this work, we need to do it."

"Alright. But you listen to the team that's in place with you. If they think it's too risky or you're in danger, if they say bail, you bail."

Eleanor finished the call knowing full well she wouldn't convey that last bit of information to her handlers. If Heath knew her boss said he was in charge, he'd find a way to call off the talks now. She wasn't an idiot. If they said they needed to pull her when the hostage raid began, she'd listen to them. But she was going back in to try to make this agreement happen and free those hostages without bloodshed.

CHAPTER 25

"Not fucking happening," were Heath's first words. "You're essentially talking about making yourself a decoy while we get those hostages out. That's too fucking dangerous, Eleanor."

Eleanor looked past Heath to her team who were watching, riveted, as thought they were enjoying the latest episode in their favorite soap opera.

"Guys, can you give us a minute to talk?" She asked and then waited while they shuffled out of the room.

When she looked back to Heath, his arms were crossed, muscles bulging and eyes glowering in a stance that said "no way in hell" in no uncertain terms.

She wanted to say "you're not the boss of me," but caught herself in time.

"This is my job, Heath. And I'm good at it. You need to back off and let me do it."

His eyes flashed darker, if that was even possible.

"You weren't sent here to be a diversion for a rescue operation. You could be killed doing that."

She leveled him with a look and crossed her own arms. She didn't have the advantage of that bolstering up her arm muscles to the point of distraction the way he did but she didn't care.

"If we pull me from the talks now, he'll know exactly what's happening. And you can pull me out at the last minute, when it's too late for him to do anything about it. You'll be right outside the room when we meet and you know there's only one exit to that room. What is he going to do?"

Heath seemed to seethe and she could see he was clenching his teeth. He unhinged them long enough to yell. "What is he going to do? How about kill you? How about that?"

His team came in behind him but she ignored them. She had faith in Heath's ability to take care of her. This was a man who'd grown so much from the boy she once knew. He was sharp and strong and so damned capable. There was none of the wild kid who used to bluster his way through shit.

This man knew how to keep her safe. She was sure of that.

Now she had to convince him. "He'll have no reason to do that if you don't give him a reason to. We can keep my team here if you want. Beth can come with us but I can send her back to the hotel for something so they don't suspect anything. Then you'll just interrupt and pull me out saying there's been an emergency at the last minute."

Her hands clenched in frustration. Why was he treating her like this? She had a job to do. She thought he'd have her back at that.

Merlin spoke from behind her. "We just got the call, Woof. She's going in. She gets one more shot at this agreement. Team Two will be watching the bunker. If they see the chance to go in, they'll take it and we'll pull Eleanor."

The curses that came from Heath's mouth weren't pretty.

That was okay. She didn't need him to be happy. She just needed him to let her do her job.

CHAPTER 26

"Then I believe we have an agreement, Ms. Bonham. I will release the hostages 24 hours from now and your government will give me the agreed-upon satellite images," Demir said.

He stood with several of his advisors behind him. His brother sat in the corner texting. It was where he'd been for the entirety of the talks. It was good because that meant he wasn't over at the bunker. As one of Demir's main fighters and the leader of his military forces, it helped to know he wasn't where the raid would take place if it had to happen.

Eleanor hesitated a beat at his insistence on the 24 hours, but she supposed that he wanted time to set up the exchange for the images. She wouldn't be involved in that. That handover would happen through a military team, maybe even Heath's team, after she went back to the US.

Her job was done. There would be no written document between her government and Demir. Nothing that anybody could trace back to show what the US government was doing in the region. But she'd done it. Thanks to this agreement, they would get the support they needed to shut off the weapons trade and they'd get the hostages out without anyone having to put their lives on the line.

Heath and Duff were outside the door here and Merlin had taken Beth back to the hotel, so they wouldn't be in the line of fire, but Zip and Jangles were with Delta Team Two at the bunker. She felt better knowing they would be safe now instead of headed into a situation where they could be hurt or even killed.

She nodded and held out her hand. "We have an agreement."

The watch on Demir's arm vibrated and he glanced at it before tapping something to dismiss the alert.

He grinned as he shook her hand. "Will you do me the honor of joining my brother and I for dinner before you leave?"

"I would be honored, but first I need to let my people know we have an agreement in place." If she didn't the raid might go ahead and that couldn't happen.

They stood and Farid's brother came forward. He leaned in as if he were going to speak to Demir as he'd done so many times in the last week. But this time, he turned at the last minute and grabbed her. He covered her mouth, his hand hard and unforgiving as he clamped down on her. And then she felt the bite of something in her arm.

A syringe. She wanted to kick out knowing if she could just make a sound, Heath would be in the room in a heartbeat. But someone had her lower body. She felt instantly heavy like any movement was too much. She was slogging through mud. Or cement.

She fought to move, to do anything to let Heath know something was wrong. He and Duff were right outside the door. All she needed to do was to make a noise. To knock over something.

Her body was numb and unresponsive. She watched in horror through bleary eyes as two of Demir's advisors moved the chairs they'd been sitting in moments ago and lifted a trap door in the floor.

The rug was attached to the door. Once it was closed from the inside, no one would be able to tell how she'd been taken from the room or where she'd gone.

There was no time for her to do anything to stop what was happening. She tried to fight whatever they'd injected her with but it was like fighting against a tidal wave as blackness crashed over her.

CHAPTER 27

Heath was nowhere near as calm as he needed to be for this op. He and Duff were outside the door to the room where the talks were taking place, just as they had been countless times this week. But his whole body physically ached to go in and pull Eleanor out of there.

She'd been right that if they stopped the talks, Demir would have been suspicious, but still, it didn't mean she should be in there putting herself at risk.

Fuck, he hated this.

Still, Zip and Jangles were with Trigger and Lefty and the guys at the bunker. They'd tip them off the minute they made the decision to move and they'd give them time to get Eleanor out. He trusted them. Team Two was a good team.

He tried to relax his muscles. His arm was nearly fully healed and the little pinches of pain he felt from time to time were easy to ignore. Which was good. He needed to be ready for anything right now if he was going to keep Eleanor safe.

Their comms crackled as the channel opened and he heard Zips' voice in his ear.

"Something went wrong. We're taking fire from inside the bunker. Get Eleanor out of there. Get her out, now!"

Heath didn't need to be told twice. He and Duff turned and Duff got them into the room with a boot to the door.

The empty room.

Heath moved in, weapon raised, heart slamming out a panicked rhythm in his chest.

She was gone. Fuck, she was gone! How the hell was this happening?

Zip spoke again. "We're taking the bunker. Clear out of there."

Heath was cursing up a blue streak as Duff answered. "Eleanor is missing. Going after her."

The words gutted Heath. The room had no windows and no other door. He knew they didn't have much time before the fighting broke out here, too. Demir's soldiers were all over the compound. They'd be coming for them as soon as they found out about the raid at the bunker.

"Watch our six," he said to Duff as he lowered his weapon and started scanning the room for the way out.

There. The chairs that had been in one corner

earlier now stood in front of the large desk on the other side of the room.

He went to where they had been and checked the rug. "Trap door," he said to Duff who came to provide cover as he lifted the door.

They looked down into a tunnel that was dimly lit. At the bottom, he could make out a shoe. Eleanor's shoe.

His mind screamed as he tried to figure out how long ago they could have taken her. Had he heard anything from inside the room? Maybe something his mind had automatically dismissed as normal, but that might have been her trying to call out for him.

His gut churned and nausea hit as he thought of her trying to call to him and not getting the help she needed.

Duff gave him a nod and Heath lowered himself into the tunnel, raising his weapon. Duff dropped down after him, pulling the trap door shut. With any luck, Demir's men would think they'd left and wouldn't follow them down the tunnel. They needed to find Eleanor and get her out safe.

They had to. He couldn't begin to think about any other ending than that.

"I'm coming for you, Nori," he said under his breath as he moved. "Hang on. I'm coming."

CHAPTER 28

Eleanor groaned as someone slapped her again.

She was surprised to see it was Demir. Her mind was fuzzy and she wasn't seeing straight, but she'd expected Farid to be the one hitting her not Demir.

"Traitorous American whore. Were the talks even real or was this all your government's distraction?"

Eleanor tried to speak but couldn't. Besides, he was partially right. She had been sent in as a distraction. But she'd genuinely hoped she could end this without any gunfire.

What had happened to make him take her like this? And would he release her?

A sob tore from her chest at the thought that she might never get out of here. Heath would come for her. Of that she had no doubt. But would he get killed in the process?

They were in an underground tunnel. It was carved

out from the rock and only caged bulbs lit the area, not doing a very good job of it.

She was tied to a chair in an alcove along the tunnel. Would they wait here? Is this where she would be held while they negotiated her release? Would they negotiate?

Her mind was quick to provide memories of terrifying videos of hostages being beheaded. She felt sick.

But they hadn't hurt the doctors and they had been ready to release them. Surely they would negotiate for her.

But the rage in Demir's eyes was undeniable. Whatever was happening, it was bad. He looked wild with anger. And not at all like he was thinking clearly.

Terror coursed through Eleanor and she watched as Farid and Demir's advisors tried to pull him back from her.

He shook them off. He held a gun in one hand but he reached out and slapped her hard again. "She's going to tell us all she knows."

Farid was there pulling on his brother's arm again. "We need her alive if she's going to be any use to us. If they breach the bunker and get Asil, we need to have a bargaining chip to get him back."

Eleanor tried to focus her mind. How far had they taken her? Would Heath be able to track her or had she been out for hours?

"I will get my son back!" Demir raged.

What was he talking about? Eleanor knew Demir

had a son named Asil and another named Vadik. She hadn't seen either at the compound and had assumed they weren't there.

The drugs pulled at her mind, threatening to pull her under again.

Then time slowed as Farid looked at his phone, his face going white at whatever he'd read there.

"What is it?" Demir demanded, turning away from her. Eleanor's head lolled and she tried to straighten up. To look around. That was what she should be doing, right? Looking for a way out.

She couldn't lift her head.

The cry she heard next was guttural and raw. The sound of heartache.

It came from Demir. She opened her eyes in time to see him spin as he raised his gun.

Time slowed and she knew there was no getting away from this. There was no way for her to stop what was about to happen. Still, her instincts screamed at her to move. To try to live. To do all she could to get out of the way of those bullets.

She shoved herself to the side, trying to throw herself over and out of his way. It didn't work. She felt the chair tip but she was too late.

He shot her. Once, twice. Pain seared her stomach. It spread. It was everywhere and all encompassing. And it drowned her, swamping her in pain so strong she couldn't breathe. Couldn't move.

There was shouting and running and then all was

quiet as she struggled to suck air into her lungs, struggled against the agony that overwhelmed her. She gasped for air, but her body was losing the battle to stay conscious.

She tried to focus on Heath. On the thought of him coming for her. It broke her heart to know he would find her like this. That he was too late. It would gut him and she hated that.

The pain was too much and she gave in as blackness engulfed her again.

CHAPTER 29

Heath heard gunshots ahead of them in the tunnel and felt his heart freeze in its tracks in his chest. They were far ahead of where he and Duff were. Too damned far. He couldn't get to her to stop whatever was happening.

He moved, powering through the panic and fear, knowing if Eleanor was hurt, he needed to get to her. He needed her to be okay.

He'd been an idiot to think he could be with this woman again and not let his heart get involved. So damned stupid. His heart was in this and then some.

If he let himself imagine what might be happening to her up there, he wouldn't get through this. Instead, he kept his head on target and his flashlight and weapon on the tunnel ahead of them.

Duff had his back as they moved. He still didn't know how they'd get out of here once they found her.

The compound was likely still teaming with Demir's men.

But Demir and his brother had run so maybe his men had, too.

Zip broke through on their comms. "We've got the hostages. Bugging out."

Duff gave Zip an update on their progress in the tunnels and listened to Zip curse on the line.

He kept his head on the goal. Keep moving ahead. Get Nori. Get her out safe.

Keep moving ahead. Get Nori. Get her out safe. He would repeat that damned mantra again and again until they had her.

He slowed as he saw light up ahead and listened. He and Duff pressed to either side of the tunnel.

"Any movement?" Duff asked.

"Nothing." Heath could make out a widened portion in the tunnel, almost wide enough to be called a room. And in the light of the bare bulbs that hung suspended above it, he could make out a crumpled figure in a chair.

His heart wept. It was the only way he could describe the despair and hopelessness that flooded him. He knew that was Eleanor. And she wasn't moving.

"Got you covered," Duff said and they began to move. The space ahead of them was clear.

As they approached, Heath looked in either direction to be sure there were no alcoves or anything that could have a surprise in the form of people or explosives.

It killed him not to drop his weapon and run to Eleanor's side. But if they got themselves killed, they couldn't save her. And if he was sure of one thing, it was that he was going to do everything in his power to save Eleanor.

They swept the area and only when they were sure it was clear, did he kneel by her side as Duff stood sentry above them, weapon ready.

Heath's heart couldn't take the sight before him as he got her out of the chair and laid her down. Eleanor was bleeding from a shot to the stomach and a shot to the hip.

Her eyes opened and she moaned as he lay her on the floor. It was about to get a lot worse. And it gutted him to know he was going to cause her pain, but he had to stop the bleeding.

He grabbed quickclot from his pack, balling the material and pushing it into her wounds as she screamed. He had to do this, but it killed him to hear the pain wracking her body as he pushed the lifesaving material into the holes that asshole had put in her body.

He couldn't lose her. Not now.

"I'm so sorry, Nori. I'm so sorry. I just have to get these packed and then we're going to get you out of here."

He followed this with sterile gauze, balling that and

packing them into the wounds again and again before dressing them with a sterile covering and taping that into place. She had passed out by then, her brow sweat-dampened from the pain.

The caliber of the weapon had been small and he sent up a quick prayer in thanks for small favors. Then he lifted her and started to run.

He could hear Duff behind him and Zip came on comms. They were in the compound clearing out the few remaining soldiers from Demir's army. Maybe the man didn't want to start an all-out war because he had ordered his army to retreat when he ran. That or they'd simply run off on their own. It was hard to say.

When Heath hit the end of the tunnel, Jangles was there with Trigger and Lefty to pull Eleanor up for him. Now he only prayed they could evac her to a hospital in time to save her. Because if Eleanor didn't make it, he didn't know how his heart would either.

CHAPTER 30

Heath had slept fitfully next to Eleanor's bed the last few days but he gave up and sat watching her now. The rest of his team had gone back to their new base in Killeen a couple of days after Eleanor checked into the DC hospital after her emergency surgery in Turkey.

He'd begged a week off from his commanding officer and was planning to put in for more. Her step-father and his wife were staying at a nearby hotel and coming to see her every day, but Heath wanted to be there for her when she went home.

For now, she spent most days sleeping and was still heavily medicated for the pain. There were tubes and wires all over her. The bullet to her abdomen had punctured her stomach so she was on huge doses of intravenous antibiotics to prevent sepsis.

The other bullet had damaged her hip bone. It wasn't shattered, but it was bad enough that she'd be getting a brand-new hip in a few days when her body was ready for another surgery.

Heath felt his phone buzz in his pocket and lifted it out to check the screen.

Jangles. The guys had been calling to check on her every day.

Heath stood and went out the door, standing just outside of it so he'd hear her if she called out to him. Her stepdad and his wife were out getting lunch and taking a turn showering and changing clothes so he didn't want her to wake up alone and be frightened.

"Hey Jangles," he said when he'd connected the call.

"How's she doing, Woof?"

It was the standard question the guys asked.

Heath scrubbed a hand over the new growth of hair on his chin and cheek. He needed to shower and shave something awful. "She's resting. Seems to be having fewer nightmares but I can tell she's in a lot of pain. She's trying to hide it but it's bad."

Jangles cursed, echoing Heath's feelings.

"Anything they can do for that?"

"Besides the morphine? Not much. Once she gets the hip replaced, she'll be able to start walking and they think that will actually help with the pain some. I'm not sure how that works, but that's what they tell me. She's going to have a lot of PT though. It's not going to be a short road."

He still needed to figure out how he was going to be there for it all. He had forty days ordinary leave he hadn't used yet and he'd banked another one hundred days special leave he could use. He hated to leave his team for that long, but Nori needed him. And he had to admit to himself, he was in love with her. He needed to be there for her. He needed to help her through this, even if that meant leaving his team temporarily.

"How are you doing?" Jangles asked.

Heath sighed, rubbing his eyebrow with his thumb, wishing he could rub away the headache that had been dogging him for hours.

"I fucked up, Jangles," he said, hearing the emotion thicken his voice. He wasn't the kind of guy to spill about his feelings easily, but he needed to get this out there. It had been eating him up for days as he watched Eleanor pay for the aftermath of his screw up.

"How do you figure that?" There was protective indignation in his friend's voice.

"She shouldn't have been in there. You know it and I know it. I let my feelings for her get in the way of my judgment. I fucked up."

"Her boss okayed her going in. What were you going to do? You didn't have a choice. None of us did."

"Bullshit. We were on the ground here. We could have overruled her boss. Should have. But I knew how important her career was to her so I sent her in there knowing it was a bad move."

Jangles wasn't having it. "Oh hell no, man, you don't get to put this on you. We all could have said no. None of us did."

Heath felt his temper rise with his voice. "Were you standing outside that room when she was grabbed? Did you fail to hear a fucking thing when they were pulling her down into that hole? Was it you that didn't get to her in time when she was shot?"

"Woof, you got to her. You got her out of there and she's okay now. She's going to get through this and so are you."

Heath didn't answer. He shut his eyes tight and prayed again that she'd make it. He loved her. He needed her, more than he ever thought possible. He needed her to be okay with a desperation he'd never felt before.

And that left him feeling helpless. He wanted to fix this for her. Wanted to take away the pain. To make this all better for her. To erase everything that had happened down in that tunnel.

"Woof, man, don't do this to yourself. She needs you to be there for her right now. And if you're busy beating the shit out of yourself, you're not truly giving her what she needs. Let it go and focus on getting our girl up and out of that bed."

Heath nodded, even though his buddy couldn't see him. He would at least do that for Eleanor. He would make sure she got out of that bed and made it home.

CHAPTER 31

Eleanor closed her eyes and willed away the tears. Morphine couldn't begin to dull the pain she was feeling. Her heart ached as she listened to Heath. It wasn't only his words. It was the change in him. She'd seen it in the last few days.

He was no longer the confident sure soldier who had gotten her through the hell she'd gone through in Kazarus. He was sounding more and more like the boy she'd known years ago. Filled with doubt and self-loathing. The only difference was he wasn't trying to hide it from the world with jokes and bravado like he had as a kid.

She hated thinking she'd done that to him. She'd brought up all the worst memories of that last year in high school and now she was affecting him in ways she hadn't imagined.

She felt more than heard him enter the room and he was by her side in a heartbeat.

"What is it, Nori? Are you hurting?"

She nodded because it was all she could do. She couldn't speak right now. Her throat hurt with the effort of trying to hold in the emotions battling her.

He put the little switch in her hand that would let her up her pain med dose and heaven help her, she pushed it. Not because her wounds hurt. But because she couldn't face the pain of knowing she needed to say goodbye to this man again. She wanted the oblivion that the medicine would bring.

That made her weak and she hated that. Hated knowing she was running like this, but she needed to stop the feelings for just a short while. She needed to close her eyes and pretend this wasn't happening. Needed to make all of this go away.

CHAPTER 32

Eleanor's stepdad, Bill, stepped from the room as Heath was coming back with coffee.

When he'd left to grab lunch, Eleanor had been awake and more coherent than she'd been in the last few days. He could see her head was more clear and she didn't have the pinched lines near her eyes that had come from the pain. The hip surgery had gone well and the nurses were prepping her for a transition to a rehab center in the next few days.

"Hey, Bill. Is she sleeping?"

He had hoped to get back before she closed her eyes for a nap again but he was happy to sit by her bed and watch her sleep if that's all he could do. He just wanted to be close to her.

Something about the look the man gave him slowed Heath's steps.

"She wants to talk to you, son. We've set up the

rehab center and they're going to move her tomorrow. She wants to say thank you and goodbye."

Heath froze, the blow to his chest feeling like a physical one.

"Goodbye?"

He'd heard the man wrong. Or her stepdad didn't realize how close he and Eleanor had become. Didn't get that he wouldn't be leaving her side any time soon.

The man sidestepped. "Why don't you go on in? I'll wait out here."

Heath's stomach clenched and turned to acid as he clutched the coffee cup in his hand. He couldn't drink it anymore. Something told him this wasn't some misunderstanding of Bill's. Eleanor was about to send him away.

But why would she do that?

He walked into the room, putting the cup on a side table before turning to face Eleanor.

She was propped up in the bed and was smiling at him. It was a fake smile. He knew it to his toes.

"Hey," he said. It was lame but it was what he had. He crossed to the bed. He'd just talk her out of whatever the hell she was about to say. That was all there was to it.

She swallowed. "Hey." There was a heartbeat where he thought she might give him a genuine smile and everything would go back to how it was between them. To how it should be.

Then she spoke and it passed. Hope passed.

"I want to thank you for all you did for me, Heath."

He took her hand and sat by the bed but she didn't grip his hand back. Her hand sat in his.

"I'm going to be moving to rehab tomorrow. They say I'll be there a month. Maybe a little less."

"I've got leave time saved up—" he started but she was shaking her head.

"You've done enough for me, Heath. You'll never know how grateful I am, but I can't ask you to stay here any longer with me. You've done enough for me."

Now he shook his head. "I wanted to do it. I want to be by your side through this, Nori. Look I know I said it couldn't be anything more than a temporary thing, but I was an idiot. I don't want this to end, Eleanor. I want to be with you. Now that we've found each other again, I don't want to let this go."

She looked away from him and he froze.

"But you don't want that," he said, realization dawning. He was such an idiot. She hadn't wanted more than what they had in Kazarus. He'd been the only one hoping for more.

Hell, she had probably been wondering why he was still hanging around.

She looked back to him. "I want to put all this behind me, Heath. I don't want to remember what happened over there."

Her words hit him like a sledgehammer to the chest and he thought his heart might just give out right then and there.

He was such an idiot.

"So, that's it, then." He said, his words laced with the shock that was coursing through him. How had he not seen this coming? How had he so misread her?

"Thank you for all you did for me, Heath."

He nodded at her words and stood, his motions stiff and awkward.

"Yeah," he said, and he threw a smile he wasn't at all feeling onto his face. "Well, you know. Here to serve and all that."

He winked at her and turned away. He didn't want to see her reaction. Couldn't watch the pity that would enter her eyes if she realized he was reeling from the blow of her telling him she didn't want more with him. He couldn't take pity from her.

He should say something more. Do something more. But he couldn't. He couldn't speak. He could only walk woodenly from the room, fighting to keep from breaking down and begging her to tell him why she didn't want him. Why she didn't feel the same incredible connection he felt between them. The connection he'd felt when they were younger. The one that had never, in all those years, gone away.

CHAPTER 33

Heath was going through the motions of a night out at The Ugly Mug with his team, but it was just that. He felt dead inside.

He barely tasted the beer in his hands. Nothing tasted good. In fact, nothing had any taste at all. And every time he let himself think, Eleanor was the only thing that he could focus on. The look on her face when she told him goodbye.

He wanted nothing more than to throw himself into the next mission or at the very least a solid PT session. Physical training was what his body needed to forget everything that had happened with Eleanor. To forget how much he wanted her and that she would be lost to him for good this time.

Instead, his team was going to be at the base for the next few weeks. He'd been pissed when Trigger and the guys got a callout while he and his team were left home sitting on their asses, but at least that meant he didn't need to watch those guys with their women at the bar.

It was shitty of him to be so fucking jealous of their happiness, but there it was.

His team had been assigned to do their five-year renewal of Code of Conduct Certification to cover COC applications in wartime, peacetime, and governmental or hostage detention environments. Which meant being deskbound in a classroom with a lot of time to think about what Eleanor was going through without him.

He couldn't stop himself from wondering how she was doing. He wanted to know if she was hurting. How her recovery was going. If her career had been hurt by what had happened out on the mission.

Not that it was her fault that the analysts back home had decided Demir couldn't be trusted. Not that she could have known Demir's team would somehow get tipped off to the fact a Delta team was watching the bunker, ready to raid and rescue the hostages.

But still, technically her negotiation had been a failure and that left a sour pit in his stomach knowing that he'd been part of that.

He stood, grabbing his beer as Jangles and zip looked up at him.

Jangles looked like he was about to say something when Duff entered and wove through the tables to the booth at the back where they sat.

"PT tomorrow." Duff was as stingy on the words as he always was.

Zip was the first to respond. "No code of conduct?"

Duff shook his head. "Merlin needed a few personal days so Roe gave him the time, pushing back our code of conduct certification. We get a reprieve for a few days."

Rouvin "Roe" Turano had been their commanding officer for the last eight years. He was a good guy most of the time so it wasn't a surprise he'd give Merlin time if he needed it.

"Mer ok?" Zip asked.

Duff gave a nod and went to the bar.

Heath didn't need to be told twice.

He drained the rest of his beer and put the empty on the table, heading for the exit. He would go back to the base and spend a few hours on the obstacle course before he turned in. He could beat himself to a bloody pulp on that thing if he tried hard enough. And he planned on it.

CHAPTER 34

Eleanor looked at her computer screen, not really seeing it for the second day in a row. She had been working remotely a few hours a day from her private room at the rehab center. Not that she was expected to. She was on medical leave.

But she needed to keep her mind busy. Needed to keep herself from having to think about Heath. She had been thinking they might somehow work out a way to stay together even with her career and home being in Washington and his in Texas. She'd wanted that so damned much it made her heart ache.

But she had seen what being in his life again had done to him and she couldn't handle that. She wouldn't bring him back to the place he'd been when they were teens where he second guessed himself.

He was a confident elite forces special operative

and he deserved that. Deserved all he'd earned the hard way.

A nurse stepped into the room.

"Eleanor, you have a visitor."

Eleanor's heart flipped, doing a somersault right there in her chest. She wanted to see Heath walk through that door. Wanted to see those sea green eyes look at her again. Wanted to somehow have it work out between them.

"It's Merlin—says he's one of your boys." The nurse was fanning herself. "He's hot!"

Eleanor forced down the disappointment that it wasn't Heath and put her computer on the side table.

The door opened and Heath's teammate walked in wearing dark BDUs and a tight-fitted T-shirt that should have merited some appreciation from her. The man was good-looking, to say the least. Tall, broad, and muscular with a smattering of gray hair that only made him sexier.

He did nothing for her. Not that she wasn't happy to see him. She would always be grateful to the men who made sure she and her team got in and out of Kazarus safely. There would always be a special place in her heart for those men.

She wanted to ask how Heath was. But part of her didn't want to know. If he wasn't missing her the way she was missing him, that would gut her in a way she didn't think she could handle.

"I hope it's okay that I interrupted your day."

She smiled. "Any time. Having a break from rehashing the Kazarus disaster isn't something I'll complain about."

They were still going over the events that had led to her injuries at her office, as much as she and her boss tried to argue there was no other way things could have gone.

They hadn't known about Onur Demir's son and his illness. It was something that changed the entire landscape of the negotiations. They were still trying to figure out who had been gunning for her to stop the negotiations and how the forces inside the bunker had been tipped off that the Delta team was on their doorstep ready to raid the place.

They had gotten answers to why Demir had lost it and shot her down in that tunnel, though. His son had been killed in the raid. It was a fluke. The machines responsible for keeping him alive had been hit and damaged. He couldn't survive off of those machines.

Merlin grimaced. "That bad, huh?"

Eleanor shrugged a shoulder. "I'll survive."

She had a feeling he wanted to ask more and she would bet it had to do with whether her career would survive or not, but he didn't ask the question and she didn't offer an answer. The truth was, she would make it.

The deputy director was latching onto what had

happened, arguing against negotiating with guerrilla forces in the future. He was riding this high, trying to use it to push his agenda and career forward for all it was worth.

But as far as her boss was concerned, Eleanor had done her job. It was just that the people looking at all the data back here in Washington had analyzed things differently than she had. She would bet Merlin and his team dealt with that kind of thing all the time. Where the people on the ground weren't necessarily the ones getting to call the shots. It was part of the job.

She sat back in her chair, forcing herself not to ask about Heath. "What brings you here? Follow-up from the op?"

Merlin shook his head, no. "This is a personal trip."

Her brows went up but other than that she gave no reply.

Merlin looked nervous and she had to admit there were some humor in seeing this big man looking anxious. He shifted in his seat. "Heath doesn't know I'm here."

Eleanor was surprised by how much those words hurt. She supposed in some small way she had been hoping maybe he had sent him. How stupidly sophomoric of her was that? Like they were in high school and passing notes through friends.

Besides, she was the one who'd sent Heath away. She had no business hoping for news from him.

Merlin leaned forward putting his forearms on his

knees and watching her intently. "He would kill me if he knew I was here, but he's not the same since Kazarus."

Didn't she know it. That was the reason she'd sent him away. But how could she explain that to this man? She didn't want to hurt Heath any more than she already had and she definitely wouldn't discuss his loss of confidence in himself with someone else.

"I appreciate you coming here and telling me that, Merlin, but Heath and I aren't right for each other." She tried to force a smile, but she couldn't. It hurt too much. "He and I just aren't…" She didn't know how to explain this to him. "We just aren't meant to be together. We weren't back in high school and we aren't now."

"I think you're wrong. We all saw the way you two were together. Hell, you couldn't ignore that. None of us would admit this easily, but we want that with someone. We want what you two feel for each other."

Eleanor turned and looked out the window. It was all she ever wanted and she hoped someday he found the happiness he was looking for. She didn't have the strength to let Merlin see how hard it was for her to admit that she wasn't going to be that for him. So instead she looked out the window and forced herself not to cry.

They didn't know how Heath had been before he entered the military. They couldn't have seen the signs she had. The way his faith in himself had taken hit after hit with her back in the picture. The way he'd regressed to someone she knew he never wanted to be again.

She wouldn't do that to him. No matter what his teammate thought he needed.

CHAPTER 35

"Roe, you got a minute?" Duff stepped into their commanding officer's office.

He hoped his CO wouldn't care that he was going to ask for a couple of days' time when Merlin hadn't gotten back yet from his personal time. The truth was during their down time between missions, they could usually take off for R&R, but with their certification being due they all needed to be here to get that done.

But he'd seen the way Heath was pushing himself these last few weeks, as if the devil was chasing him. Duff might not be the most sensitive guy in the world, but he knew Heath was hurting. And the truth was, Duff would do anything for any of the guys on his team. These guys accepted him for who he was and didn't treat him like the freak that a lot of people saw when they looked at him.

"Come in," Roe said, looking up from his paper-work. "What's up, Duff?"

"Listen, I know we've got to get this certification done, but would it be okay with you if we push it back another couple of days? I need to make a quick trip."

* * *

Duff had looked up Eleanor's information on the way to DC. He wasn't surprised to see her pushing herself hard in the physical therapy room at her rehab facility, sweat forming a sheen on her skin as she pushed herself to walk between two parallel support bars.

Heath's Nori was one of the most committed people he'd ever seen.

It was why what had happened to her sucked. She deserved more than what happened at the end of that negotiation.

Eleanor looked up as he approached. "Duff! What are you doing here?"

He gestured to a chair near the apparatus, even though it looked like it could easily collapse under his weight.

She nodded to his unspoken question and he lowered himself carefully into the chair. The nurse assisting her helped her into a wheelchair and pushed her over to where he waited.

And then he tried to think of what to say. He wasn't the kind of guy who came up with the right words easily, or knew how to say them in the right way. He'd probably screw this up, but he had to try.

Maybe he should tell her how Heath looked the last few days. It wasn't pretty. So maybe he wasn't right to start with that.

"Heath doesn't know I'm here."

She was nodding at him. "And you probably didn't know that Merlin has already been out to see me."

"Oh." That stopped Duff. Merlin had only told Duff he needed to take care of something personal and that it wasn't a big deal or anything he should be worried about. It hadn't occurred to him that Merlin had already come out here to see Eleanor.

"What did he say?" When the words left Duff's mouth, he immediately wanted to call them back. He wasn't any good at this.

Eleanor smiled at him and it was the kind of gentle smile that said she understood he was trying. Heath would have been so damned lucky to have this woman in his life. Duff wanted to make that happen.

"What did you want to say to me?" Eleanor asked. And again there was understanding in her tone. Understanding and patience.

"He's miserable." Duff scrubbed the back of his head. "I've never seen him like this. Heath bounces back, you know?"

Eleanor's eyes were sad. "I don't. We haven't been a part of each other's lives for a lot of years now. Too many years, I think. We're in different places now."

Duff might not be the most sensitive man on the planet, but he knew she wasn't talking about the distance from DC to Fort Hood.

He looked around the restaurant, not sure what to say. He should have asked Zip to come with him. Or Jangles. They would know what to say.

Eleanor rescued him, raising a hand to wave over the nurse. "Have lunch with me, Duff." She smiled at him. "I owe you guys at least that much for all you did for me and my team."

Duff shrugged and looked away. None of them ever knew how to handle people thanking them for their jobs the way they did. But he would enjoy having lunch with Eleanor. Besides, his flight back to Fort Hood wasn't until that night.

And maybe if they had lunch, he could think of something to say to convince her that Heath needed her. Maybe he could find a way to get her to see him again. If she could just see Heath, she'd have to see they were meant for each other, wouldn't she?

But as they moved from the rehab room to the dining room in the large facility, she started talking about other things. About Washington DC and all the good food there, about the physical therapists and how they thought they could have her home in another couple of weeks, about a movie she'd watched before.

It was clear she was finished talking about Heath.

CHAPTER 36

Heath looked up to find their CO heading straight for them out on the field. He, Merlin, and Duff were marching with full packs and gear in the hot Texas sun and had been for the last two hours. He was planning to go another two or more before quitting.

But Roe didn't look like he was fucking around. Heath wondered if maybe they were getting called back out on a mission.

He was wrong. It had nothing to do with a mission.

"The next one of you fucking assholes that comes into my office and asks to put off your recertification is getting my boot up his ass and a month of restrictions. Are we clear?"

Merlin and Duff looked a little guilty, but two of them asking for time off wasn't usually enough to get Roe riled up.

Heath looked around and realized Jangles and Zip

209

hadn't joined them yet. Shit, maybe those two had asked for time, too.

Roe didn't wait for an answer since none was needed. His word was law. "The new re-cert requirements on the Code of Conduct aren't optional and they aren't something anyone on the chain is fucking around with. Your team is confined to the base until it's done."

Roe turned and walked off and Heath looked to Merlin and Duff. They only shrugged.

Damn, it looked like tomorrow he'd have to give up his strategy of beating the fuck out of himself, and instead sit in front of a computer watching training videos and taking tests.

Fucking fantastic.

He started moving again, picking up to a 4 mile per hour pace instead of the typical 3.5 mile per hour clip they usually marched at. If this was his last day of burying his head in pain and exhaustion, he was going to make the best of it.

With any luck, maybe he would sleep hard enough that he wouldn't be plagued by dreams of Eleanor tonight.

CHAPTER 37

It was almost humorous when Eleanor picked up her phone and saw a video call coming in. She found Jangles and Zip looking at her from a small room on the other end of the feed. Except she was too tired to laugh.

It had been days since she'd gotten a good night's sleep. She cried most nights and when she did finally fall asleep, she tossed and turned as Heath tortured her in her dreams.

Not that he was actually torturing her. No, in her dreams, what she felt were his kisses, his arms around her, his eyes on her. But when she reached for him, he wasn't there.

Just like he wasn't there in real life.

It was stupid, really, that she was so upset over not having him in her life. She hadn't had him since the day she told him to get out and leave her alone when she was seventeen. That had been hard, but this was even worse. She hated that he wasn't part of her life anymore. Hated that she couldn't pick up the phone and hear his voice or his laugh. That there wasn't any need for them to figure out a way to visit each other and make a long-distance relationship work.

Eleanor looked at Jangles and Zip. For once, Zip wasn't smiling.

"He misses you, Eleanor," Zip said.

Jangles nodded. "He's not the same man he was before the Kazarus mission."

Eleanor wasn't strong enough for this. Because despite the fact it seemed his whole team wanted her to know how much he missed her, Heath hadn't once reached out to her. He seemed to know as well as she did that this had been the best move for both of them.

She tried for a smile, but she could tell it probably came out all wrong. And damn if she didn't feel herself losing the battle with tears. She was losing that battle more and more, it seemed.

"You know, guys, I love you all for trying to help. It was really nice of Merlin and Duff to come out here."

"Merlin and Duff were out there?" Jangles asked and he and Zip shared a look of surprise.

She didn't answer. She was so tired. So over-whelmed by everything. And she was beginning to doubt her decision. Maybe she'd been wrong to send Heath away, but it had killed her hearing him doubt himself the way he had.

She lost the battle with her tears now. She swiped at her cheeks with the back of her hand.

Jangles looked distinctly uncomfortable but Zip stepped closer, like he wanted to reach through the screen to her and she loved him for that. These men were all so important to her now. They'd gotten her and her team through the hell of Kazarus.

"Aw don't cry, Eleanor. I know he's thinking about you. He might not have come there yet, but I'm sure he wants to."

Jangles stepped up then, too. "We're on lockdown. He's not allowed to leave the base until we finish some training we've been putting off."

She shook her head. "And when did that order come?" Merlin and Duff had clearly gotten off base, so the order was probably new.

Jangles looked abashed. "Uh, yesterday."

The door behind the two men opened and her heart slammed to a stop when she saw Heath come in. He was mid-sentence asking what was keeping the other two men when he saw her on the screen.

She didn't know what she hoped for but it wasn't the way his face went completely blank and still. And it wasn't the way he turned and walked from the room without a word.

She pressed her lips together not wanting to say anything because if she did, she knew she would be bawling in front of these men and there wouldn't be a damn thing she could do to stop it. The pain that sliced through her heart at seeing him turn and walk away was too much.

She had started to doubt her decision, but it looked like he hadn't been.

Jangles and Zip looked pained too.

Zip tried to make it better. "Nori, he's—"

She shook her head stopping him. Hearing Heath's nickname for her was too damned much. She cut the video feed and put her phone face down by the bed. She couldn't talk to them anymore. Couldn't see the pity emanating from them.

Until very recently, her career had been everything to her. It was what got her up in the morning, what drove her to work longer hours than anybody in the office including her boss, and what kept her coming back. It was the drive to be the best she could be at what she had chosen to do.

And right now it meant absolutely nothing. She had realized how utterly hollow her life was. She swallowed down the large lump in her throat and brushed away any remaining tears as she turned on her side and hugged her knees to her chest in bed.

Her chest felt tight and the heartache pushing on her seemed like it might swallow her whole. Everything hurt. She was going to have to try to cope with the fact that she'd lost Heath Davis forever. That was something she didn't know how to do.

CHAPTER 38

If Heath thought he was stupid back in high school, he hadn't come anywhere close to the idiocy he had demonstrated with Eleanor.

Seeing her face on the video conference screen— no, not just her face, her tears— had destroyed him. He should have stayed when she insisted he go. He should have seen through whatever it was that had made her send him away. Should have been there for her when she needed him.

He didn't know if he could get her to talk about why she'd sent him packing, but at the very least he was going to go there and try like hell. He was going to tell her how much he loved her, and how sorry he was he hadn't been enough for her.

He went back to the room they'd been working in, watching those stupid code of conduct training videos

215

for the last three hours, and grabbed his bag. Jangles and Zip trailed him down the hall and were now standing in the doorway watching him as Merlin and Duff stared back at him from their seats.

"It's about damn time you're going to her," Duff said, surprising them all.

Jangles looked at all of them. "Uh, I hate to burst your bubble Woof man, but the CO says that's a no-go."

"We're on lockdown until this training is done, remember?" Zip added.

"Yeah, I remember," Heath said. He remembered and didn't give a shit. He would take whatever punishment Roe dished out.

"You're looking at desertion if you do this," Merlin said quietly.

Heath met the eyes of the men on his team. "I gotta try. She's worth it."

"Damn right she is," Duff said.

Jangles and Zip stepped into the room. Zip was the one to speak and he was grinning again. "We got your back. We'll tell the CO you had to see about a woman." Zip was laughing at his use of the line from *Good Will Hunting*.

"The hell you will," Heath said. "If Roe finds out you knew I was leaving and didn't stop me, you'll all be in hot water. You're not taking that on for me."

Merlin stood. "Fuck off, asshole. We can take the heat, same as you. Now go get your woman."

Heath didn't have to be told twice. He ran from the

room never wanting to be somewhere faster in his life. He needed to get to Nori. He needed to make it right and tell her what she meant to him. That she was more important to him than anything. Any mission. Any assignment. Even his career.

CHAPTER 39

Eleanor thought a hot shower would be a good idea. She was wrong. It turns out when you bawl your eyes out in a hot shower, blotchy doesn't begin to describe what happens to your face.

Now she sat wrapped in a fuzzy old bathrobe in her room with a cold towel over her face. The nurse had thought she was crying over her frustration at the process of her recovery and she hadn't tried to change that perception. Truth was, her recovery was going faster than she'd thought it would. She would go home in another few days. She would have outpatient physical therapy for weeks to come and she wouldn't be running anytime soon, but she was up and moving around on her own now.

She should call a friend. She laughed. Was she kidding? She didn't have a friend. Not any real ones. She and Beth were friendly at work and she liked her a lot, but they didn't get together outside of the office. If Beth called her or she called Beth, it was to tell each other something about work.

Maybe she should get a Kindle. She could start reading romance novels so that she could at least see what a happy ending looked like even though she wasn't going to live one anytime soon. She squeezed her eyes tighter under the cold cloth. She didn't think she had any tears left but damn it, she was wrong again.

She was really getting tired of being wrong lately. Someone knocked on her door, bringing her up to a sitting position much too quickly. The rehab facility had a front desk and no one got in without a call up to let her know who was there. Not to mention, she almost never had visitors. Not unless it was someone from the office bringing her a file or something.

She looked down at her fuzzy robe and the cold cloth that was now in her hands instead of on her face. Fabulous.

She went to the door and looked through the narrow glass window pane at the side of it.

And then she yelped because Heath was standing outside her door.

"Nori?" he asked.

"Shit," she muttered and stepped back. She was so not in any condition to see him.

It wasn't only that she looked like shit. She just

couldn't do this. She couldn't get up her hopes again and have them dashed.

For so long, she had put memories of Heath Davis behind her only to have him walk back into her life in a time and way she never could have imagined.

And it hurt like hell knowing he was even more incredible now than he'd been back in high school. He was a man of heart and strength and courage. A man who fought for his country and what he believed in. She'd never known a better man than him.

And she'd sent him away.

"I know you're in there, Nori. I saw you."

She pressed her lips together, capturing them between her teeth as though maybe she could somehow be quiet enough to convince him she wasn't here.

"You realize I can get in there if I want to, right?" He paused and she could picture him assessing the situation. "I can pick the lock, of course. Or I could just take the whole damned door off its hinges."

Her phone rang and she stupidly looked at it where it sat next to her bed like that would somehow tell her who was calling.

Heath went quiet on the other side of the door and she thought maybe he was trying to call her.

She crossed the room to lift her phone and looked at the screen.

It was Merlin. She'd given him her number when he visited.

"Hello," she said quietly after swiping the phone to answer it and putting it by her ear. She was speaking as though she might still be able to play possum and pretend she wasn't in the room.

"Eleanor, it's Merlin. Heath is on his way there. I wanted to let you know you should open the door for him. He didn't ask me to call, but you should know he left the base against orders to come to see you."

He seemed to be waiting for her response, but she didn't know what to say. She wasn't an idiot. She knew that leaving the base against orders was sure to get you into a lot of trouble.

"You there, Eleanor?" Merlin said on the other end of line.

She gripped the phone with both hands. "I'm here. He's at the door now."

"Let him in, Eleanor. Please. Hear him out."

Eleanor hung up the phone and turned to face the door. She didn't know if Heath still waited on the other side or if he'd given up.

But she walked slowly toward it. She'd made a mess of things but maybe they could fix this. They were still both headed in completely opposite directions, but at least maybe this time they could say a proper goodbye instead of the way she'd left things.

She opened the door, only then realizing she was still in the fluffy robe with her hair pulled back in a sloppy tail and no makeup on her face.

Heath stood in the doorway, looking a little surprised to see she had opened it.

"Hi." *Wow. Eloquent, Eleanor.*

"Nori," He breathed. He looked wrecked, pain evident in the lines on his face and the sorrow that filled his eyes.

Tears came to her eyes at the sight of him there. She couldn't stop them. He was here in front of her and there was so much she wanted to say to him. But she didn't know how to say any of it. She didn't know how to do this.

"Shhhh. Don't cry." He reached for her and pulled her to him and she could feel how gentle he was being as he enclosed her in his arms.

"You came," she said.

"You were crying. Of course I came."

She leaned back and tilted her head up to look at him. "What?"

He brushed the back of his hand down her cheek. "On the video call with Zip and Jangles. You were crying. So I came."

She cried harder at that and his arms went around her again as he shushed her. He lifted her and walked to the armchair in the corner of her small room at the rehab facility. When he settled into the chair with her in his lap, he brushed the tears from her face.

She didn't want to know what she looked like.

She was worse than a wet, soggy tissue with the way she kept crying but she couldn't help it.

"Shhh, don't cry, Nori. Please don't cry."

As Heath held her, there was hope sliding into her chest now and she didn't know if she could handle that. But God, how she wanted it. Wanted him. Wanted a future and possibility and all that came with giving herself to the only man who'd ever been able to claim her heart.

"Tell me why you sent me away."

His words hit her heart hard but she forced herself to tell him the truth.

"I heard you talking on the phone. You'd started doubting yourself again like you did when we were younger."

He shook his head. "You heard me doubting myself and that made you send me away?"

She took a deep breath. "When we were younger, you always looked like you knew what you were doing, like you were the king of the high school and no one could knock you down."

He snorted. "Hardly."

"Yeah, well that's the thing. I saw through that. I knew it was an act back then. You were insecure about a lot of things."

He touched her face again like he couldn't help the contact. "You always did see through me. You saw it all."

"When I met you again back in Turkey, you were such a different man. It was clear from the minute you found me at that airport that you were damned good at what you did and you knew it. Not in an arrogant way. Just in a way that said you had no doubt in your ability to keep me safe. To get the job done. And it was clear your teammates knew that, too. They trusted you even when it was clear we had a history."

He kept his gaze locked on hers. "I didn't keep you safe." His voice broke at the words and tears came to her eyes again.

She was causing him so much pain. She hated that. "That's just it. It wasn't your fault I got shot. It was my decision to go in there. And my boss approved it. You didn't make that call, Heath. I did. And I'm not sorry if it meant you and your team had the time you needed to get those hostages out of the bunker without anyone getting hurt.

"But when you came back from that mission, you were different. I saw all the old doubt in your eyes again. I heard you talking to your teammate about how you'd failed. I couldn't take that. I didn't want to be responsible for bringing you back to that kind of thinking."

He dipped his head, touching his forehead to hers. "Yeah, I doubted myself after that mission but it wasn't the first time and it won't be the last. Me and my team are all confident in our abilities but we all second guess ourselves sometimes. We just have each other's backs. If one of us is having a hard time, the other guys pick up and make sure we get the job done.

"But none of that changes how I feel about you. I

love you Nori. I don't think I've ever stopped. There was just too much guilt getting in the way of my feelings when we were younger. I thought the best thing I could do was clear out of there after what Jason did and leave you alone. But I know now that you're the only woman I could ever love. Now that I've found you again, I never want to walk away."

She didn't answer. She just wrapped her arms around him and kissed him, trying to put all she was feeling, all the love she had in her heart for him into that kiss.

When they broke apart, he met her gaze. "Tell me that's yes. Tell me we can try this even though we're in different cities and we're both basically slaves to our work. Please tell me we can give this a shot."

She nodded. "We don't have a choice. I love you. There's no other choice but to make this work."

He let out a whoop and lifted her, fluffy bathrobe and knotted hair and all, and spun her around.

She didn't think it was possible for her to feel any lighter than she did now, any happier.

And then he kissed her and she knew she was dead wrong. His arms around her as he kissed her was everything she ever wanted in her world. Everything she didn't know she so desperately needed.

When they kissed, it was like they'd never been apart. Not just now and not all those years ago when things had first gone so horribly wrong.

"You're so beautiful, Nori," he whispered against her

lips. "I've never wanted another woman the way I want you. Never felt like this with anyone."

She smiled. "Ditto," she said quietly. She had been with other men after him but nothing had compared. When Heath touched her, it felt so right.

"I know you're not ready to make love yet, but I want to touch you, to look at you."

He grinned wickedly and leaned in, whispering all the things he wanted to do to her in her ear. Eleanor whimpered and squirmed in his arms. She might need to try to convince him she was healed up enough to do at least a few of those things. Maybe the one where he bent her over ….

"When you're well," he said, running his hand over her shoulder as though he could read her mind.

"Promise?"

"Cross my heart."

She snuggled into his arms and let her heart soak up the fact he'd come for her. He loved her.

"I can't believe you came because I was crying."

"Always," he said again and she believed him. She knew there would be times when he couldn't do that. She was realistic about his job and the fact he could be called away at any moment and not even be able to tell her where he was going or when he'd be home.

The truth was, she could be moved any moment to a new post. They'd need to figure all that out as they went along. But not being with him was no longer an option. Her heart couldn't stand that.

"I need to go back to my base and take whatever punishment my CO has for me."

She ran a hand over his chest. "Merlin said you left after your CO told you not to. You shouldn't have done that. You could have called."

He was shaking his head. "Not good enough for my woman. I wanted my arms around you. I wanted to hold you and stop the hurting."

She tilted her head back and looked in his eyes. "I don't deserve you."

He huffed a laugh and shook his head. "You deserve a whole lot better than me but I'll have to do."

CHAPTER 40

Eleanor didn't know how Heath had convinced his CO to let him come back a week and a half later when she was discharged from the rehab center, but she didn't care. He'd been home with her for three days now and it had been heaven waking up beside him each morning.

Even if he did insist on sleeping over the covers so he wouldn't be tempted to make love to her at night until she was ready for it.

At his pace, though, he'd keep her waiting for months and she wasn't having that. She was still moving a little slowly, but she could handle having sex and she wanted her man.

She stepped from the shower and drew on her robe, knowing she would find Heath in the kitchen with coffee and breakfast ready for her.

Whatever he'd made was about to get cold, if she had her way.

She towel dried her hair then left it loose and padded down the hall to the kitchen.

As she approached, she undid the belt at her waist and let her robe hang open at the front.

Heath had his back to her at the stove. His muscles bunched as he stirred whatever was in the pan. His T-shirt was stretched taut over hard muscles and she couldn't help but ogle at him, letting her eyes travel over the large bulge of his biceps. Her hands tingled with the need to pull that shirt off him and run her hands over his warm skin.

She was wet already. If she couldn't manage to seduce him, she was going to lose her mind. This was the worst part of being shot. The waiting to have him touch her again.

She almost laughed at herself. How quickly she'd forgotten the terror and pain of that time in the tunnels with Demir. But Heath did that to her. He took away the fear and pain and kept her grounded here in the moment with him instead of back in the horror and memories of that underground nightmare.

Heath glanced over his shoulder at her, then turned away, putting his hands to either side of the stove and letting his head drop.

She heard him cursing under his breath.

Good. She was getting to him.

She walked to him and put her hands on those

shoulders. God they were so hard, so damned strong. Just touching them had her wanting to press herself against him. She stepped closer, letting her body melt against his.

He cursed again and she laughed. She heard him flick off the burner and move the pan off the stove before he turned.

And then he had her.

"Are you sure you're ready for this?" he asked, his hands gripping her shoulders as he waited for her answer.

"More than sure," she whispered. "Please, Heath." It was plea and prayer wrapped in one. She needed this man. Needed the connection of making love to him. Of knowing he was hers and she was his. That the years of being apart were gone.

He used the fabric of her robe to pin her arms in place as his head came down and he captured her nipple in his mouth. Having him hold her in place increased the erotic sensation and she pressed herself forward, wanting more as she moaned her response.

He went to the other nipple and sucked, then nipped with his teeth and she was lost. She felt herself growing wet for him as her body throbbed in response to his teasing.

"I want to touch you," she panted out, wriggling to try to escape the way he'd wrapped her in the cloth.

His response was to lift her and carry her to the bedroom where he lay her back, still not loosening his hold on her arms as he trailed his mouth down her body to her belly. And then she was breathless and moaning when his mouth went lower, covering her mound, his tongue laving her clitoris in teasing circles.

He let go of the fabric now, loosening his hold on her arms as he brought his hand down and added his fingers, bringing the pleasure between her legs to a fevered pitch.

She pulled her arms up and wrapped them around his shoulders then up the back of his neck, running her fingers through that too-long hair.

She gripped him tightly as she writhed beneath him. She wanted their bodies together, closer than this, as close as they could be. But he didn't stop and she couldn't stop the plea escaping her lips as she orgasmed, muscles clenching around his fingers.

The orgasm crashed through her, wave after wave of sheer pleasure made all the more powerful because of the emotion she now knew they shared. Her love wasn't one-sided.

And as he drew out the bliss of her orgasm she let herself believe that maybe this time they could make forever happen.

Heath knew he would never tire of seeing Eleanor fall apart in his arms. She was flushed and beautiful laying spread out for him.

LORI RYAN

She tugged at his shoulders, pulling him up. "I want you inside me, Heath. I need to feel you inside me."

He stilled as he realized he didn't have a condom with him. "I don't have protection."

She smiled and there was a wicked teasing to the light in her eyes. "Haven't I told you that you don't need to protect me? I've got condoms in the drawer."

He growled and opened her bedside drawer while she laughed.

When he came back to her, he hovered above her, sharp gaze drawing her eyes to his, capturing them and holding her there. She had to hear him. Had to know he meant every word of what he was about to say. "I will always protect you, Nori. Always. You'd better get used to that because I love you. I'm in this for good and you might not love the way I show that love all the time. I'll be overbearing and bossy when it comes to keeping you safe. I'll be a jealous ass when we're out in public. I'll tell you I love you all the time and demand the same from you."

She tilted her head back and laughed. "I think I can handle you, big guy."

God he wanted to hear that sound forever. "I love making you laugh almost as much as I love making you come."

She blushed.

"And blush," he added. He could do that forever, too, he thought.

He set her down in the bed and stretched out beside

her, watching her long lithe legs as she turned and reached for the condoms.

It was so damned wrong that he felt jealous of whoever she'd bought them for, but felt better when she had to tear open the box to get one out. At least she'd never used them with the other guy.

When she handed him a condom from the package he took it but put it aside. He wanted to lay with her, touching her, feeling what it was like to be with her again, reveling in just being with her.

But she put her hands on him, running them down his chest. And then her mouth joined her hands and he was lost.

"Nori," he groaned.

She moved her mouth across his skin, her tongue fluttering out to tease him, making him think he might lose control before he even got inside her.

What the hell was that about? He had always been able to control himself, but fuck if she didn't make him feel like he was anything but in charge of his body.

She lowered herself and he knew seconds before she did it that she was going to take him into her mouth. His cock was already so goddamn hard he didn't think he could take it, and when she slid her hot mouth over him, his whole body jerked.

He looked down and found her looking up at him as she sucked. The image was more than he could handle. He pulled her over and flipped them so he was on top of her. She laughed but it was breathless and he knew the teasing had gotten to her just as much as it got to him.

He had a condom open and on him in seconds flat and then he was burying himself in the warm heat of her body.

He stopped, holding perfectly still inside of her as he rested his forehead on hers. "I just need a minute."

She whimpered and moved her hips and it was all he could do to grit his teeth and hold on, making sure he didn't come before she did.

He put a hand to her hip holding her still. "Don't move, Nori."

She laughed now, low and sexy and so damned amazing.

He moved his hand to find her clit between them and teased, feeling her muscles tighten around him.

"Oh God, Heath, please. Please, I need more."

He let go, moving then as he drove into her and he felt her orgasm take hold of her just as he began to come. It was embarrassing how little control he had with her, but he couldn't stop himself as he pounded into her and she cried out, gripping his shoulders and urging him on.

When they lay sated together afterward, he kissed her temple and closed his eyes, sinking into her hold. Being apart from her had been too hard and it was something he'd never do again if he could help it.

CHAPTER 41

Two weeks later, Heath was still pulling extra duty and he had two more months of reduced pay to look forward to, but he'd been lucky. Roe had handled his violation locally instead of letting it be handled up the chain of command.

And extra duty and lost pay were fine by him. Eleanor would be arriving later tonight for the weekend and he couldn't wait to see her again. Their last visit in DC had been too damned short.

For now, he was sitting in The Ugly Mug, a bar next to the firing range owned by BF, a former airman who made sure the beer prices were cheap and the jukebox was always working. It was the kind of place that had three spots outside reserved for combat injured veterans. That pretty much said it all as far as Heath and his team were concerned. It was their kind of place.

From what Heath had seen, BF's manager, Kelle,

was the one who kept everything running smoothly at the bar while BF ran the firing range.

"Woof, what time is Eleanor getting in?" Jangles asked, taking a handful of corn nuts out of the bowl on the table they'd commandeered at the back of the room. It was in a dark corner and they liked it that way. People tended to leave them alone more if they couldn't see them as much.

Heath couldn't stop the grin that spread over his face. "Three hours." Which meant he'd be heading to the airport in one to be sure he didn't miss her. It was overkill, but that's how he rolled where she was concerned. He was coming to accept that.

"Lucky bastard," Zip said, his usual smile in place to soften the words.

Heath only grinned wider. He was a lucky bastard. He'd almost been stupid enough to let her go. Thank God he hadn't.

He saw Trigger and Lefty walk in, their women on their arms. Heath had been so fucking jealous of them only a month ago and now he only smiled wider at the sight of them so fucking happy.

He and his team had spent months with Lefty's woman, Kinley, protecting her while she testified against a serial killer. She'd been so damned strong through all of that and it make him happy to see her back with Lefty with all of that behind her.

She reminded him of his Nori with her strength and tenacity. He checked his watch again. Not time yet, but soon. He didn't know how Lefty had waited seven months to be with Kinley.

Kinley tugged Lefty's arm toward where Heath and his team sat and Trigger and Gillian followed. Gillian was an event planner who was in the wrong place at the wrong time on a hijacked airplane but she stayed strong through all of it and ended up helping to trip up the terrorists and take them down.

As they all stood to greet the newcomers, Heath realized it took a really strong woman to be with them. He hoped the other guys on his team found that soon. It was sappy and cheesy as fuck, but he didn't care. He wanted them to find the kind of love he had for Eleanor. The kind of woman who was strong enough to return that love.

Merlin was headed their way. The look on his face had Heath looking up. Grim didn't begin to describe it.

Fuck, if they were about to be deployed, he'd have to cancel with Eleanor and she had already boarded her flight. That was the life she'd signed on for, but he still hated for it to happen so soon after they'd finally figured out how much they wanted to be together.

"What's up?" Jangles asked as they all turned to Merlin.

Merlin waited until Trigger, Lefty, Gillian, and Kinley had moved away to a table and then leaned in, speaking low enough that they wouldn't be overheard.

"We just got word." He looked to Zip. "Someone's

been trying to track you in some dark places. The analysts think it might be Demir."

Shit. Demir had to know it was their group that was responsible for the raid on the bunker, but during debrief Zip had told them his mask had come partially off when they freed the hostages. They were hoping nothing would come of it, but if Demir had locked in on Zip to blame for his son's death and was trying to hunt him down, that was some bad shit.

"We got your back," Jangles said to Zip and the rest of the group nodded. It went without saying, but they all wanted him to know anyway.

The doctors and nurses had been able to explain a lot of why Demir had been acting the way he had.

He hadn't kidnapped the medical staff simply because the opportunity to grab them presented itself when they crossed his path during a mission with a medical charity.

He had taken them because his son was sick. From what they'd been told, there was very little possibility of a cure for the type of leukemia that had plagued the young boy. Demir had been told it was unlikely the ten-year-old would survive to see eleven but he'd been desperate to save him no matter the cost.

He had been forcing the doctors to try a controversial experimental method of treatment that none of the doctors and nurses thought would help.

The theory was that Demir had very much wanted to come to an agreement of support with the US government but he was trying to delay discussing the hostages because he was convinced they could help his son. The doctors had shown Demir improvements in the boy's bloodwork, and the improvements had been real.

Unfortunately, the doctors had known they wouldn't last. It was typical of someone with his condition to appear to be doing better just before death. But the doctors and nurses had known if they were still Demir's prisoners when his son died, it would end poorly for them.

So they'd used the improvement to convince Demir he could release them and were banking on the hope he would do so before his son's condition took a turn for the worse.

Merlin looked to Zip. "He's right. We've got your back. The analysts are monitoring the situation. They'll let us know if they find out anything more. In the meantime, your info is locked down. Whether it's Demir or someone else looking for you, they won't find you."

Zip nodded, fixing a smile to his face, but for once Heath wondered if it was genuine or not. He knew Zip had been beating himself up over the mistake and finding out that having his face exposed like that might actually lead to trouble had to be hard on the guy.

Heath raised their empty pitcher to one of the bartenders, Jake, signaling for a refill. Then he pulled some bills from his pocket and placed them on the table.

"This round's on me, guys."

"You heading out?" Merlin asked.

Heath nodded. It hadn't been an hour yet and he'd end up with a ton of time to kill at the airport, but maybe he'd stop and get Eleanor some flowers. He was too damned eager to see her to sit there any longer.

Duff grunted. "Say hey to Eleanor for us."

Heath grinned. Sure, he could do that. Maybe after he'd said hey to her himself a few times.

Eleanor saw him when she was halfway down the escalator and wondered if her heart would always do that little flippy thing for him. He stood looking up at her, more handsome in dark jeans and a button-down shirt than any man had a right to look.

Then she saw he was holding a small bundle in his arms. She couldn't make out what it was until she drew close and he pulled the little ball of fur from the crook of his shoulder and held it out toward her.

"Isn't he adorable?" he asked.

Eleanor laughed. The puppy was small. Maybe only a few pounds, but the chocolate brown and tan fur sticking out in tufts was making up for the lack of mass.

He held up the dog. "He's probably got some yorkie in him, or maybe silky."

She reached out and pulled him to her. "You know we would be the worst dog owners on the planet. We're each called away from home at a moment's notice and we work long hours when we are home."

"I know," he grinned and leaned down to kiss her, stealing her breath for a moment with the heat of it.

When he pulled back he shrugged. "I went to buy you flowers and I found this little guy in the parking lot so I brought him instead. I was thinking I might see if the guy who owns the bar we hang out in wants him. BF could use a pet."

She tilted her head at the dog. "Didn't you say Ris and Nan are retiring soon? Maybe one of them can take him?"

Heath shook his head grinning. "I think your idea of retirement for a Delta is different than ours."

His buddies would be working for HALO Security, a private security and protection company that, last he heard, had started taking a lot of kidnap rescue jobs. They wouldn't have quite the danger and workload of a DELTA team, but they weren't going to be sitting behind a desk.

Eleanor snuggled the dog closer as Heath took her bag off her shoulder and carried it for her, slinging one arm around her as they walked.

"He's so cute," she purred.

Heath laughed. "You totally want him."

"I do," she said. "I could send him to doggy daycare during the day and when I come to visit you here, he could ride with me. He'd certainly fit under the seat."

"Doggy daycare?" He laughed harder.

She swatted at him. "It's a thing."

When they made it to his car, he got her settled in and then ran around to the driver's seat. He put one hand on her leg as he drove. The little dog snuggled in her lap and put a paw over Heath's hand.

Damn, he could get used to this. It sucked they had to be in two separate states for now, but he wouldn't ask her to give up her career for him. They would make it work.

"I have news," she said, running her hands over the puppy's small head.

"Yeah?" he asked.

"Your team is going to get word of this tomorrow, so I'm not telling you anything that won't be shared with you or that's above your clearance," she started.

He looked over at her but then back out at the road as he navigated the airport traffic.

"What's that?" he asked.

"They've made an arrest at State." He could tell from the sadness in her tone that this was hitting her hard and he tightened the hand on her leg.

"Who was it?" he asked, knowing she was talking about the person who leaked information on her itinerary.

"Deputy Director Hughes. He didn't sell the information, but he wanted the talks to fail. They found texts on his personal phone. His belief that we needed to go back to the days of never negotiating with hostage takers was strong and he thought if he could sabotage the talks, people would start to see things his way."

Heath cursed as his hands clenched the wheel. He wanted to tear the man's entrails from his body and watch while he bled out. His personal mission to change policy had put Nori in danger. Hell, he'd done more than that. He'd gotten her shot.

"What did he do?"

Eleanor continued to pet the puppy as it lolled in her lap. She was handling this better than he was.

"He let the information about my flight slip to someone he knew would sell it to people who might want to stop the talks. Ironically, he was also the one who made sure your team was sent there to protect me. I think he thought he could keep me safe and make sure it was nothing more than a close call. He was hoping that would be enough to stop the talks. I guess he didn't bank on them putting a tracker on me and keeping up their efforts after the fact."

"Do they know who the information was sold to? Who was behind all the attempts to stop the talks?"

"It was Barrera. At least the first few attempts were Barrera. Some of the analysts think the attack when we left the compound that day might have been Demir himself, trying to slow down the talks to give

LORI RYAN

his son more time before he had to give up the doctors."

"What do you think?" Heath asked. He trusted her gut on that more than analysts who weren't face to face with Demir.

"I think it's entirely possible. Demir was torn right from the start. That's what made him so hard to read during the negotiations. I think he truly believed in his cause and what he was trying to do for his country. But his family is also enormously important to him. Family is everything for a man like Demir. He wanted to save his son, but he also wanted the talks to work for his cause. In the end, he didn't save either of them."

"He still has his army and more supporters than most groups in his position. He's still got a real shot at taking over the country and ousting the King."

Eleanor nodded. "He does. I don't think the US can trust him, but he'd probably be better for the people of Kazarus than the current regime."

Heath didn't like the sorrow in her voice so he brought the conversation back around to something that would make her smile. "What are we naming our new puppy?" It was clear she was keeping the little stray.

She studied the puppy. "Maybe Bruno."

Heath tipped his head back and laughed. "That's a lot of name for such a small fry."

She only smiled back at him.

Heath looked at the dog, dividing his attention

244

between the dog and the road. "Maybe Norbert. Or Squeak."

She drew the dog up to her chest. "Quiet. If you keep that up, he'll figure out he's tiny." She wrinkled her nose. "He needs a bath."

"And food and a bed. A collar and tags."

As much as Heath thought he would have wanted nothing more than to run straight home and get her in to bed—and he did—he liked this. Liked planning for their future, even if, for now, that was only sharing a dog together and flying back and forth to see each other whenever they could.

Because having her in his life meant he finally had more than just work and the mission and his team. He had her love. And that was everything.

* * *

Trent's heart skipped a beat at the sound of Destiny's voice. He would recognize that sweet voice anywhere. Even in this crowded bar. He spun around and spotted her quickly. She was sitting at a booth with several other women. The table was littered with shot glasses, both full and empty.

Though he'd known Destiny most of his life, she hadn't looked him in the eye or intentionally spoken to him in twelve long years. She'd never been far from his mind in all that time, but he'd never had the balls to approach her.

"Zip?"

Trent jerked his gaze back toward his Delta team at the sound of his nickname coming from Woof.

"Have you heard a word I've said?" Woof asked.

Trent drew in a breath. "No. Sorry. I see someone I know. I need to speak to her." He couldn't fathom why he thought that would be a good idea. Destiny had never given a single indication she would appreciate him approaching her in over a decade. Nevertheless, he slowly made his way toward her.

The past rushed back to slam him in the chest as he stepped between bar patrons at the Ugly Mug. Flashes of her laughing when they were children and she first moved in next door to his family. The time they snuck out of their houses late at night to catch lightning bugs. Evenings sitting at his mother's kitchen table doing homework.

Those were the happy times. And the two of them had not been alone during those years. Trent's twin brother, Sean, had been there too. The three musketeers. They'd been the perfect balance until Sean asked her out on a date and ruined their dynamic. Nothing had ever been the same after that.

"Des," he breathed out when he reached the table.

Five women looked up at him. Their faces were a mixture of emotions. They knew exactly who he was even though he'd never met them. Interesting.

"You must be Trent," the dark-haired, petite woman said.

"I am. And you are?"

"Libby." She smiled broadly and sat up as tall as her small frame could. "This is Christa, Bex, and Shayla." She pointed at the rest of the women as she spoke.

Trent nodded politely at each of them.

The blond, who he thought was called Christa, spoke next. "We work together."

"For the airline. Open Skies," Libby added.

Trent nodded at each of them and shifted his gaze to Destiny. "Do you have a few minutes? I'd love to catch up." This might possibly be one of his worst plans ever. For one thing, she might shoot him down in front of everyone. It wouldn't surprise him. For another thing, he knew he was opening a wound by confronting her. They'd gone their separate ways after Sean died. It had been too hard to face each other.

No. That wasn't true. Trent would have liked to have talked to Destiny after the funeral. He'd have given anything to have her even glance at him. But she'd ignored him entirely.

He'd understood. She'd been hurting. Her fiancé was dead, and seeing Trent had undoubtedly caused her more pain. But he'd been hurting too. He'd lost his brother. His best friend. Maybe the two of them could have healed and moved on faster if they'd had each other.

He swallowed, trying to force all this emotion to the back of his mind.

It looked like Destiny was about to tell him to fuck

off, but one of her friends stood, pulled her from the booth, and forced her to face him. Destiny swayed on her feet, and he decided several of the empty shot glasses on the table had been consumed by her.

He took her arm to steady her, hoping this confrontation wouldn't be the worst plan ever. "I'll bring her back to you in one piece," he told her friends as he led her away from the security of her posse.

Trent slid his hand down to grasp hers, and he wove through several people until they reached a corner. The noise level was lower in this spot. Destiny looked very nervous.

Taking a deep breath, Trent met her gaze. Even after twelve years, she still made his heart race. She was just as sexy. Just as cute. Her smile could slay him. It was time to face her. He'd missed her terribly. Whatever her reasons were for cutting him off, he wanted to hear them. If she told him to take a hike, he'd have to accept it. But he needed to get her to talk to him. If he didn't, he would regret it for the rest of his life.

Be sure to pick up the second book in the Delta Team Three series to find out more about Trent and Destiny's Delta by Becca Jameson.

And if you haven't read the rest of the books in the series, I've included the links for all five stories.

Nori's Delta by Lori Ryan
Destiny's Delta by Becca Jameson
Gwen's Delta by Lynne St. James
Ivy's Delta by Elle James
Hope's Delta by Riley Edwards

*

Also, thank you so much for reading Nori's Delta! I hope you loved Heath and Nori as much as I loved writing them.

Remember Ris and Nan, two of the guys who got Nori's team to her? They'll be moving over to Lori's HALO Security Series! Look for the first book, Dulce's Defender SOON!

ABOUT THE AUTHOR

Hi! Thank you for reading my books. I hope you'll check out some of the other series I've written several including the Heroes of Evers, TX, Sutton Billionaires, and HALO Security Series. I love grabbing readers and taking them into a gripping world with the heroes and heroines I've come to love. If you feel like you're seeing old friends when you enter her books, I've done my job.

I live in Austin, TX with an incredibly patient husband, three children who amaze and amuse me every day, and two dogs who sometimes behave but mostly don't (which is mortifying since I used to be a professional dog trainer). There are rumors there might be a leopard gecko joining the menagerie soon if my son can keep up his chores and save enough money for the tank and whatnot.

You can reach out to me at www. loriryanromance.com or join my reader group at https://www.facebook.com/groups/ 397438337278006/. I'll see you there!

There are many more books in this fan fiction world than listed here, for an up-to-date list go to www.AcesPress.com

You can also visit our Amazon page at: http://www.amazon.com/author/operationalpha

Special Forces: Operation Alpha World
Christie Adams: Charity's Heart
Denise Agnew: Dangerous to Hold
Shauna Allen: Awakening Aubrey
Brynne Asher: Blackburn
Linzi Baxter: Unlocking Dreams
Jennifer Becker: Hiding Catherine
Alice Bello: Shadowing Milly
BP Beth: Scott
Heather Blair: Rescue Me
Anna Blakely: Rescuing Gracelynn
Julia Bright: Saving Lorelei
Cara Carnes: Protecting Mari
Kendra Mei Chailyn: Beast
Melissa Kay Clarke: Rescuing Annabeth
Samantha A. Cole: Handling Haven
Sue Coletta: Hacked
Melissa Combs: Gallant
Anne Conley: Redemption for Misty
KaLyn Cooper: Rescuing Melina
Liz Crowe: Marking Mariah
Sarah Curtis: Securing the Odds

Angela Nicole: Protecting the Donna
MJ Nightingale: Protecting Beauty
Sarah O'Rourke: Saving Liberty
Victoria Paige: Reclaiming Izabel
Anne L. Parks: Mason
Debra Parmley: Protecting Pippa
Lainey Reese: Protecting New York
TL Reeve and Michele Ryan: Extracting Mateo
Elena M. Reyes: Keeping Ava
Angela Rush: Charlotte
Rose Smith: Saving Satin
Jenika Snow: Protecting Lily
Lynne St. James: SEAL's Spitfire
Dee Stewart: Conner
Harley Stone: Rescuing Mercy
Jen Talty: Burning Desire
Reina Torres, Rescuing Hi'ilani
Savvi V: Loving Lex
Megan Vernon: Protecting Us

Delta Team Three Series
Lori Ryan: Nori's Delta
Becca Jameson: Destiny's Delta
Lynne St James, Gwen's Delta
Elle James: Ivy's Delta
Riley Edwards: Hope's Delta

Police and Fire: Operation Alpha World
Freya Barker: Burning for Autumn

Julia Bright, Justice for Amber
Anna Brooks, Guarding Georgia
KaLyn Cooper: Justice for Gwen
Aspen Drake: Sheltering Emma
Deanndra Hall: Shelter for Sharla
Barb Han: Kace
EM Hayes: Gambling for Ashleigh
CM Steele: Guarding Hope
Reina Torres: Justice for Sloane
Aubree Valentine, Justice for Danielle
Maddie Wade: Finding English
Stacey Wilk: Stage Fright

Tarpley VFD Series
Silver James, Fighting for Elena
Deanndra Hall, Fighting for Carly
Haven Rose, Fighting for Calliope
MJ Nightingale, Fighting for Jemma
TL Reeve, Fighting for Brittney
Nicole Flockton, Fighting for Nadia

As you know, this book included at least one character from Susan Stoker's books. To check out more, see below.

SEAL of Protection: Legacy Series
Securing Caite
Securing Brenae (novella)
Securing Sidney
Securing Piper
Securing Zoey
Securing Avery
Securing Kalee (Sept 2020)
Securing Jane (Feb 2021)

SEAL Team Hawaii Series
Finding Elodie (Apr 2021)
Finding Lexie (Aug 2021)
Finding Kenna (Oct 2021)
Finding Monica (TBA)
Finding Carly (TBA)
Finding Ashlyn (TBA)

Delta Team Two Series
Shielding Gillian
Shielding Kinley (Aug 2020)
Shielding Aspen (Oct 2020)
Shielding Riley (Jan 2021)
Shielding Devyn (May 2021)

Shielding Ember (Sep 2021)
Shielding Sierra (TBA)

Delta Force Heroes Series

Rescuing Rayne (FREE!)
Rescuing Aimee (novella)
Rescuing Emily
Rescuing Harley
Marrying Emily (novella)
Rescuing Kassie
Rescuing Bryn
Rescuing Casey
Rescuing Sadie (novella)
Rescuing Wendy
Rescuing Mary
Rescuing Macie (Novella)

Badge of Honor: Texas Heroes Series

Justice for Mackenzie (FREE!)
Justice for Mickie
Justice for Corrie
Justice for Laine (novella)
Shelter for Elizabeth
Justice for Boone
Shelter for Adeline
Shelter for Sophie
Justice for Erin
Justice for Milena

Shelter for Blythe
Justice for Hope
Shelter for Quinn
Shelter for Koren
Shelter for Penelope

SEAL of Protection Series

Protecting Caroline (FREE!)
Protecting Alabama
Protecting Fiona
Marrying Caroline (novella)
Protecting Summer
Protecting Cheyenne
Protecting Jessyka
Protecting Julie (novella)
Protecting Melody
Protecting the Future
Protecting Kiera (novella)
Protecting Alabama's Kids (novella)
Protecting Dakota

New York Times, *USA Today* and *Wall Street Journal* Bestselling Author Susan Stoker has a heart as big as the state of Tennessee where she lives, but this all American girl has also spent the last fourteen years living in Missouri, California, Colorado, Indiana, and Texas. She's married to a retired Army man who now gets to follow *her* around the country.

www.stokeraces.com
www.AcesPress.com
susan@stokeraces.com

Made in the USA
Coppell, TX
15 October 2024

38688605R00154